We Love Animals
Daffy Down Donkey

We reached Daffodil's field to find that she was standing in exactly the same place we had left her yesterday afternoon.

"Oh, Daffodil!" I cried, and I clambered over the fence and ran to her without even thinking about Jilly, left there with Mud on his leash.

Daffodil felt stiff all over, as if her bones had frozen. Her head was way down and even when I stroked her she didn't lift it.

"Quick!" I yelled to Jilly. "Come and help me!"

Also available in the We Love Animals series:

Daffy Down Donkey

Jean Ure

First edition for the United States and Canada
published by Barron's Educational Series, Inc., 1999.
Copyright © Jean Ure, 1998
All rights reserved.

First published in Great Britain in 1998 by Scholastic Children's
Books, Commonwealth House, 1–19 New Oxford Street, London
WC1A 1NU, UK

A division of Scholastic Ltd

All inquiries should be addressed to:
Barron's Educational Series, Inc.
250 Wireless Boulevard
Hauppauge, NY 11788
http://www.barronseduc.com

International Standard Book No. 0-7641-0969-3

Library of Congress Catalog Card No. 98-48464

Library of Congress Cataloging-in-Publication Data
Ure, Jean.
        Daffy down donkey / Jean Ure.
           p.   cm.— (We love animals)
        Summary: Jilly and Clara join the "Animal Lovers," an
        organization dedicated to preventing cruelty to animals,
        and try to save a neglected, sick donkey.
        ISBN 0-7641-0969-3 (pbk.)
        [1. Donkeys — Fiction. 2. Animal rescue —Fiction.
        3. Animals — Treatment — Fiction.] I. Title. II. Series:
        Ure, Jean. We love animals.
        PZ7.U64Daf   1999   98-48464
        [Fic]—dc21   CIP
                                            AC

Printed in the United States of America

987654321

Chapter 1

It was Mud who discovered the donkey. We'd taken him on an extra-long walk, Jilly and me, because it was Saturday morning and in the afternoon we were going into town with Mom and Benjy, leaving poor old Mud on his own, which he hates.

"So he has to have a really *good* walk to make up for it," I said.

Jilly agreed.

"Let's take him somewhere he's never been before. He'd like that."

He did! We took him up to Daffy Down, and Mud went mad chasing rabbits and other wildlife. We could hardly keep up with him! In the end, we just sank down exhausted onto a fallen tree trunk and watched as he raced in circles.

"It ought to be called Bunny Down, not Daffy Down," I said.

Strictly speaking it's Daffodil Down, but all the locals know it as Daffy. Old Mrs. Cherry, who lives on our lane, says that in the springtime it's a mass of what she calls "daffs." Right now, it was like one big doggy playground. I'd never seen Mud so excited! He was galloping all over the place like a big hairy spider, his nose to the ground and his tail flying out behind him.

"It's a good thing his sense of smell is all right," said Jilly.

She meant because he's deaf. Poor Mud can't hear a thing! But he can smell his dog biscuits even before you've opened the box, and Mom swears he sniffs all the cans of dog food to check what's inside them. (Benjy thinks he reads the labels.)

"He is a sort of hound," I said. Hounds always have a good sense of smell.

"*Sort* of hound," said Jilly.

We're not really sure, to be honest. These are just some of the breeds that we think may have gone into the making of Mud:

Great Dane

Irish Wolfhound

Golden Retriever

Bearded Collie

Foxhound

Deerhound

Greyhound

Whippet

Mom says he is an "all sorts," which some people think are the best. Me, for one! And Jilly, for another. We wouldn't swap Mud for a million dollars.

So anyway, we were sitting there on our tree trunk, talking about how we wouldn't swap him, "Not for *anything*," when we suddenly became aware that Mud had disappeared.

"Where is he?" wailed Jilly.

She always gets a bit nervous if she can't see him, because of course you can't yell at him like you can with other dogs.

"He couldn't have gone far," I said. "He never does."

All the same, I tend to get a bit nervous, too,

so it was a relief when we heard him start to bark.

"He's found something!" I cried. "He's calling us!"

When Mud barks like that—very high and shrill and excited—it means he wants you to come quickly and look. Jilly and I both jumped up, and went charging off to where the sound was coming from.

"There he is!" Jilly pointed. "Over there!"

Mud was standing nose-to-nose with a little brown donkey in a field. Well, the donkey was in the field; Mud was on the outside. They were nuzzling each other! It was the sweetest sight. The donkey wasn't in the least bit afraid. It was as if it knew instinctively that Mud was a kind dog and wouldn't hurt it. When it saw me and Jilly it waggled its ears, *tick-tock,* to and fro, and hung its big furry head over the fence and snuffled in our hands as we petted it.

"It's asking for food!" said Jilly, delighted.

So we both tore up handfuls of grass and held them out, and the donkey ate them greedily.

"Anyone would think it was caviar!" giggled

Jilly.

"Donkeys don't eat caviar," I said, and then hastily, before Jilly could tell me that she knew that, thank you very much, I added, "Caviar's disgusting, anyway."

"I know," said Jilly. "It's fish eggs. It's revolting."

"Grass," I said, "is a luxury. Yum yum!" And I held out another clump.

"Maybe it's because it hasn't really got any in its field," said Jilly.

We both looked at the field and for the first time I noticed how horrible it was. It wasn't really a field at all—more like a junkyard. In one corner there was a burned-out car without any wheels and a motorcycle lying on its side. A few tufts of grungy-looking grass had managed to push through here and there, and one or two patches of weedy things—dandelions and clover—but mostly it was just bare earth, covered in all this terrible clutter of old car tires and gas cans.

"That is totally disgusting," said Jilly.

She feels very strongly about people messing

up the countryside with mounds of rubbish, and so do I. I felt even more strongly about a poor little donkey having to live in the middle of it. No wonder it kept nudging at our hands for more grass! The grass that we were picking was green and juicy; not like the dry, old stuff that was growing in its yard.

"People are just so mean," I grumbled as we reluctantly said good-bye and set off back home with Mud. "How would they like to live in a horrible place like that?"

"Some people do," said Jilly.

"But it's not fair if animals have to!"

We walked in silence, back over the Down.

"It seemed quite happy," said Jilly, after a while.

"Mm. I s'pose so." I wasn't really convinced. I didn't see how a donkey could possibly be happy living in the middle of a mud patch full of old car parts.

"Maybe we'll go back and see it again," said Jilly.

"Yes." That cheered me up a bit. "We'll go back tomorrow and feed it some more grass."

I tried not to keep worrying about the donkey because, after all, we'd decided what we were going to do and it does ruin things if you're worrying the whole time. And I was looking forward to going into town! Jilly and I were going to take out an animal video from the library and then we were going to make copies of this story that had been printed in the local paper about us. We'd never been in the paper before! It was like being famous. It was all about how we'd rescued Mud.

When Muddy Four Paws was left to drown by his callous owner, he was lucky that two Riddlestone School girls were on hand to rescue him. Clara Carter and her friend Jilly Montague, both age 11, were riding their bikes along Feather Down Lane when they saw a man throw something out of his car. "At first," said Jilly, "we thought that he was dumping." But when they reached the spot, they found that what he had dumped was alive . . . shut up inside a suitcase and heartlessly tossed into a muddy ditch to drown.

And then it said how we took Mud home, but Mom said we couldn't keep him because he was too big, and so we had to give him to the End of the Line animal shelter, which almost broke our hearts, and Mud's, too. He was just so unhappy! I think he felt that we had betrayed him. It was only when Meg, at the shelter, discovered he was deaf that Mom gave in and said that we could have him. And that was only because of Benjy! Benjy is my little brother and he is deaf, too, or hard of hearing, as Mom prefers us to say.

It was Mud who really got us into the animal thing. It was because of Mud that we started helping out at the shelter, and because of Mud that we decided to become Animal Lovers and fight for animals.

This is what it said about us in the newspaper:

Thanks to the quick action of two brave girls, all has ended happily for this particular mutt, but as Jilly and Clara are quick to point out, there are plenty more animals at the shelter just waiting for someone to give them a home.

"When I grow up," said Clara, *"I am going to buy a house in the middle of a field and rescue as many animals as I can."*

And then there is this picture of Jilly and me, with Mud. Mud is all teeth and whiskers, grinning like mad at the camera, and Jilly is smiling rather sweetly the way that she does (you would never think that girl goes around calling people creeps and slimeballs!) and looking quite angelic. And, of course, *pretty*, with her little round face and big blue eyes and blonde hair, all bubbly, because she'd just had it cut.

I suppose I will have to say what I look like. I am not really sure how to describe myself. I would like to say that I am impish or elfin, as I think these would be rather nice things to be, but unfortunately it would not be true. My hair is dark and a bit straggly, and my nose is too long. It is, it really is! I wish it turned up. I have tried sleeping with my face pressed into the pillow in the hope of squashing it into a different kind of shape, but so far nothing seems to have happened. Jilly says that I am crazy and that my nose is perfectly normal. She says that people with short, stubby noses look like pigs, and while she thinks that the pig is a noble and intelligent animal, a pig is a pig and a human being is a human being.

I suppose that is one way of looking at it.

It was Meg at the shelter who got the newspaper to print our story. We were really quite surprised when they called up and asked could they come around and talk to us, and take our photograph! When our sworn enemy, Geraldine Hooper, saw it, she was just so jealous it was unbelievable. She said that I looked like a crumpled cabbage.

But I didn't care! I'd helped to rescue Mud and that was the important thing. It didn't really matter what I looked like. I made copies on the library photocopy machine to send to my grandma up north, and for my other grandma and my dad who live back in New York. Even though my dad isn't around, I knew he'd be interested. He always likes to know what I'm up to.

"So does mine," said Jilly, and she made a

copy for her dad, as well.

Jilly's dad is an airline pilot. He flies all over the world, and sends her huge exciting presents for her birthday and at Christmas. And sometimes he telephones her from faraway places, such as California and Hong Kong. Jilly gets so excited when he does this. I expect I would, too.

"I'm going to fly in my dad's plane one day," said Jilly. "I'm going to fly to America. Maybe you could come with me."

"What, and leave Mud?" I said.

"Your mom would take care of him, wouldn't she? Oh! Look! Aren't those the people that gave you the stickers?"

I looked where Jilly was pointing. I saw a table with a yellow banner saying *Animal Lovers*.

"Yes!" I said. "Let's go and talk to them."

One day about a month ago, when Jilly and I were just starting to get into animals in a big way, I'd put 50 cents in an Animal Lovers collection box and been given a yellow sticker to wear (I put in another 20 cents and got one for

Jilly, too). I'd been wanting ever since to find out more about them and see what they did. Now was my opportunity!

The same lady who had given me the stickers was standing beside the table, which was covered all over with magazines and leaflets, and petitions for people to sign.

"What are they for?" asked Jilly.

The lady said they were all "against animal cruelty."

"Can we sign them?"

"Well, I'm not sure." She looked at us doubtfully. "You're rather young."

"But we're against animal cruelty."

"We just rescued a dog," I said, and I showed her our story from the newspaper.

She read it through and was obviously impressed because she said, "Oh, that's excellent! Well done!"

"So can we sign the petitions?" asked Jilly. "*Please!*"

"I gave you money when you were collecting," I said. "I wanted to ask you what you did, but I didn't have time."

"What *do* you do?" asked Jilly.

The lady said that Animal Lovers fought "all cruelty, to all animals."

"Even rattlesnakes?" said Jilly.

"Even sharks?" I said.

"*All* animals," said the lady. "Without exception."

I racked my brains to try and think of an animal that she might not mind people being cruel to.

"Even rats?"

"Certainly even rats."

"Even . . . flies?"

"So if you found a fly in your kitchen," said Jilly, "you wouldn't kill it?"

I knew why she was anxious about this. It was because her mom had recently hung up a horrible sticky strip that if flies flew into, they died an ugly death. Jilly had told her mom it was cruel, but her mom had said that flies spread disease.

"Flies spread disease," said Jilly.

"So do human beings," said the lady.

Jilly wrinkled her brow. "So you wouldn't

kill flies?"

"No! I'd try to catch them and put them outside."

I thought this was a totally great answer and I could see that Jilly did, too.

"Could we be Animal Lovers?" I asked. "I mean, we are already, *sort* of." We'd been wearing our yellow stickers, but they were getting a bit worn by now. "Could we be real ones?"

The lady said that of course we could.

"We have a special section for junior members. Here you are!"

And she gave us each a leaflet that told you all about how to join.

"We'll do it the minute we get home," vowed Jilly.

"That would be nice. Then they'll send you a badge to wear and a sticker for your window, and you'll get a copy of the newsletter every month."

"And we can fight against cruelty to animals."

"And sign the petitions," I said. "*Please!*"

So the lady let us sign one that was against

fur and one that was against bullfighting, and I really began to feel that at last I was becoming a truly committed animal person, doing battle on animals' behalf.

Jilly asked if we could take some petitions into school, and the lady gave us two of the fur ones because she said she had a lot of those.

"I suppose you haven't got one about donkeys?" I said, suddenly remembering the little donkey in its terrible junk-filled yard.

The lady said not this time but maybe next month, and so we promised to come and see her again then.

"Because we've just found this donkey, you see," said Jilly, "and we're going to visit it tomorrow and feed it some grass."

"Because it hasn't got any," I said.

"When you're Animal Lovers," said Jilly as we walked back across the square to meet up with Mom and Benjy, "you notice things like that."

"Yes," I said, "and you do something about them."

"We'll send for our badges *immediately*," said Jilly.

Chapter 2

Mom and Benjy were waiting for us in the parking lot. Mom was a bit upset because of us taking so long, so we explained about Animal Lovers, and how we were going to join and get badges to wear.

"I hope you've got the money," said Mom.

"It's only $5," I said. "I can take it out of Julius Caesar."

Julius Caesar is my piggy bank. He is called Julius Caesar because he looks rather haughty, like a Roman emperor.

"I thought you were saving up for a new pair of sneakers?" said Mom.

I told her that new pairs of sneakers weren't important anymore. What was important was helping animals.

"What about Jilly?" asked Mom.

Jilly said that she still had some of her birthday money left, which she had been going to buy records with, but now she would use it to become an Animal Lover instead.

"Well! You're both very dedicated," said Mom.

"Yes, we are," I said, and I tried to show her some of the leaflets that we had brought with us from the booth, but Mom wouldn't look at them, she said they were too horrible, and she reached out and snatched one away from Benjy as he tried to pick it up. Benjy immediately sent up a wail.

"Dinnee big!"

He had seen a picture of a guinea pig on one of the leaflets. Benjy is mad about guinea pigs, but it would have upset him if he had looked inside and seen what was being done to them. I agree with Mom that Benjy is too young to learn about humans' hateful behavior toward dumb creatures. I think 11 is about the right age. You are old enough at 11 to face up to the horrors of the world and try to do something about them.

So we put the leaflets away, and I showed

Benjy the picture of the giraffes on the front of the wildlife video that we had gotten. It stopped him wailing, though he still prefers "dinnee bigs" to anything else. (When I was eight my favorite animal was the three-toed sloth. I hadn't ever seen one, but I just liked the sound of its name.)

As soon as we arrived home, I rushed to get Julius Caesar and shake him upside down on my comforter. I counted out $5, mostly in nickels and dimes, and took it downstairs to Mom.

"Can I have a check?" I said.

Mom groaned at the sight of all the coins, but she let me have a check for Animal Lovers, and I put it in the mailbox at the end of the lane when Jilly and I took Mud for his second walk. Just a short one, this time, but he always has two walks on weekends. He is a big dog and he needs a lot of exercise.

Jilly wasn't able to send for her badge yet, because of her money being locked away in the bank.

"Now you'll get yours first," she wailed. She was really upset about it, so I promised her I wouldn't wear my badge until she had hers. It was a bit of a sacrifice, but it's what you have to do when you're best friends with someone.

When we parted company we agreed that we would meet the next day and go up to Daffy Down again to see the donkey.

"Except we'll have to go to the shelter first," Jilly reminded me, " 'cause we gave Meg our word."

I made a face. It's not that I don't enjoy helping out at the shelter, just that I really wanted to go and see that little donkey!

"We're only sweeping out the yard," I said. "Not anything exciting, like exercising the dogs."

"Yes, I know," said Jilly, "but we *said*."

I knew that she was right: You can't let people down. Especially not when they're people who run shelters and all these poor abandoned animals are depending on you.

"OK," I said. "We'll go down to the shelter first. We could take one of the petitions with us!"

Sunday morning is the time when lots of people come to the shelter to look at the animals and see if they can find one to adopt, so Meg was too busy to talk much, but she did say how wonderful it was to be able to rely on us.

"You have no idea the number of people who say they'll come and help and then never turn up!"

I felt really guilty about this and couldn't look Jilly in the eye, but Jilly kept quiet and didn't say a word. She is so much nicer than I am!

And of course I was glad that she'd made us come, even if we were only sweeping out the yard. After all, it's a job that has to be done, and Meg said that we could leave our petition with her and that she would get people to sign it, so that was a good thing. Also, we were able to go and say hello to some of our favorite animals, although two of them, I am happy to say, were no longer there because they had been adopted. And all as a result of our story in the newspaper!

We left the shelter feeling really pleased with ourselves. Jilly said, "I know it's not very much, but at least in a small way, it's something else that we've done to help animals."

"Yes," I said, "and this afternoon we'll go up and see the donkey."

I was really anxious to get back up to Daffy Down but, unfortunately, before we could do so we had stacks and stacks of horrible homework to get through. All the time that I was struggling with it, I could hear Benjy out in the yard playing with Mud. I felt incredibly jealous!

As soon as I'd finished, and we'd had dinner, I jumped up and cried, "Mud! Walkies!" which is silly, really, as he can't hear me, but I talk to him all the time.

I'd made the mistake of telling Benjy about the donkey. I might have known he'd want to come with us! He kept saying, "Dongy, dongy!" which is his way of saying donkey. I felt a bit impatient, to tell the truth. I really didn't like the idea of having to keep an eye on Benjy *and* on Mud, but happily Mom said that she could do with a walk, too, so that was all right.

I was anxious to get going. That little donkey had really gotten to me. I kept seeing its big shaggy head hanging over the fence. I kept feeling its soft mouth nuzzling at me for food. And I also kept seeing the foul junkyard all covered in car parts. How *could* anyone keep a poor little donkey like that?

It took us ages to get up to the Down, because Benjy has these ridiculous stubby little legs and can't walk fast. But once we got there, it was really rewarding. Benjy cried, "Dongy!" and went rushing forward with Mud prancing beside him.

"Careful!" I said. "You'll frighten it."

But the donkey didn't seem frightened. It seemed really friendly and craving attention. I thought it may even have recognized us from the day before because it made these funny little wheezing sounds down its nose, almost as if it were saying hello.

"Look," I said to Mom. "It's so horrible, isn't it? Keeping a poor little donkey in a place like this!"

"It's not very nice," agreed Mom. "But maybe

donkeys aren't as fussy as we are."

I thought that was really unfeeling of her. I gave her this look and she said, "Well, don't blame me! I'm not responsible for it."

No, but Jilly and I were. We were Animal Lovers and had sworn to fight for animals.

"Let's give him some grass," said Jilly. "That's what he wants."

"Me!" said Benjy.

"All right," said Jilly. "We'll both give him some."

So Jilly and Benjy plucked handfuls of juicy grass and fed them to the donkey, while I stood scowling (because I felt that just giving bits of grass wasn't enough; we ought to be doing *more*) and Mom held on to Mud, who can't bear to see another animal eating something that he might want.

"Poor little thing!" said Jilly. "He's absolutely starving!"

"Actually," said Mom, "it's a she."

Jilly said, "How can you tell?" And then blushed at her own stupidity. I mean, for goodness' sake, she is *11*.

"I hope someone feeds her," I said.

"*We* feed her!" Benjy banged his chest, importantly. "Me and Dilly!"

"No, I mean proper food," I said.

"I'm sure they must," said Mom. "They probably come and put out hay, or whatever it is that donkeys eat."

We were all townies, even Jilly. We didn't know anything about donkeys. But it bothered me that this one was having to live in the middle of all that junk, and all by herself.

"She ought at least to have a companion! It's cruel, keeping her on her own."

"How do you know?" asked Mom.

The answer was, of course, that I didn't. It was just something I felt.

Mom shook her head.

"Clara, you can't go around righting *all* the wrongs of this world. Whoever owns her probably couldn't afford to have two donkeys."

"Then they shouldn't have one at all," I said.

"In which case, this one, perhaps, might have gone for slaughter. She might even have been rescued from slaughter. Who knows?"

"I still think it's cruel," I muttered.

Jilly and I decided that when we took Mud for his walk after school the next day we would come back again and visit her.

"And this time we'll bring her some food," I said.

"What sort of food would she like?" wondered Jilly out loud.

"Carrots," I said. I was pretty sure that donkeys ate carrots. "And apples, maybe, and . . . and bread. But I think it ought to be whole wheat."

"My, aren't we fussy!" said Mom. "Give her the best of everything! Why not?"

Well, and why not? She was a poor little donkey all on her own, and it was really upsetting me.

Chapter 3

Next day we took one of our anti-fur petitions into school and went around at recess getting people to sign it. Needless to say, Geraldine Hooper and her best friend, old No-Neck Puffin, wouldn't have anything to do with it. They just came over and sneered and said, "*Animals* again? What about people?"

Jilly said, "What about them?"

Geraldine said, "They're more important than animals."

"Why?" asked Jilly.

"Because they're human beings," said Geraldine.

Jilly said, "So what? What's so special about being a human being?"

"We can talk," said Geraldine.

"And think," said No-Neck.

"And destroy the planet," said Jilly.

That shut them up! Jilly is getting really good at putting those two in their place. All Geraldine could think to say in reply was, "I know *your* type," and go flouncing off across the playground arm in arm with No-Neck.

"People like that make me so mad," said Jilly. "They just don't *care* about animals suffering."

"No," I agreed. "They wouldn't go all the way to Daffy Down just to feed a little donkey."

"Actually," said Jilly, "I hope my mom lets me."

"Why shouldn't she?" I said.

"In case it gets dark. She doesn't like me being out in the dark."

"We'll be home *ages* before that," I said.

"Yes, and she'll go on about homework, too, I bet."

"But we always take Mud out after school!"

"Only over the road. Just for ten minutes."

That was true. It was Mom who took him for

his long walk, in the morning. After school was really just an extra.

"You don't have to *tell* her," I said.

"Then she'll get worried, when I'm not back."

"Your mom!" I said. "She's so fussy!"

"She can't help it," Jilly said gloomily. "It's just the way she is."

"Well, I'm going," I said. "My mom won't mind."

Huh! That was where I was wrong: *My* mom started on about homework, too.

"I don't want you coming back tired and skimping on your homework."

"I won't," I said.

"And I don't want you making a nuisance of yourself with that petition."

I stared at her, reproachfully. What did she mean, making a nuisance of myself?

"You called on Mrs. Cherry this morning, didn't you?"

"Oh! Yes," I said. I'd forgotten that. We'd done it on our way to school. "She signed it for us. She didn't mind."

"Well, she does now. She's worried about it, she thinks she may have done something wrong. You have to remember that she's an extremely old lady. She gets frightened very easily."

I opened my mouth to say there wasn't anything to be frightened of. All she'd done was sign a petition to stop poor little minks being gassed to death, but there are some moods of my mom's where it's wisest not to argue, especially because I wanted some food for the donkey.

Mom gave me two carrots, two whole wheat bread crusts, one apple, and some plain whole wheat crackers.

"That should keep it going," she said.

"*She,*" I said.

"She," said Mom. "And, Clara, just remember . . . I don't want you skimping on that homework!"

Jilly's mom had said that she could come so long as she was back home by 4:30—"And when I say 4:30, I *mean* 4:30"—and so we agreed that we would keep Mud on the leash to stop him from chasing off after rabbits, and us having to keep rounding him up, wasting precious minutes of our time.

I remarked to Jilly, as we set off across the lane, that we ought to find a name for the donkey.

"If we're going to keep seeing her . . . we ought to give her a name."

Jilly suggested Big Ears, but I thought that was too quaint.

So then she said, "Agatha," because she'd just been reading an Agatha Christie book.

I said, "You can't have a donkey called Agatha!" and Jilly got into a bit of a snit and said, "All right! You think of something."

So I thought and said, "What about Daffodil?"

Jilly, still moody, said, "What about it?"

"Well," I said, "it's where we found her . . . Daffodil Down."

"If you want," said Jilly.

So that's what she became . . . Daffodil.

When we reached her scrubby bit of field, she was standing on the far side with her head hanging down, looking really dejected. Some people might say, if you knew as little about donkeys as Jilly and I did, how could you tell that she was dejected? I can only reply that if you have any feelings for animals at all, you know when they are happy and when they are not. And this was one very unhappy donkey. It was really heartbreaking to see her.

We leaned over the fence and called to her, and very, very slowly she raised her head and looked across at us. I swear her eyes lit up! I'm sure she recognized us. You could almost hear her thinking (in donkey language), "These are the girls who are kind to me and give me grass."

But today we had something better! I held out a carrot and Jilly held out a roll, and Mud barked because he was excited, and Daffodil heaved a big sigh, as if making any kind of movement was a real effort for her. But she obviously wanted the food—or maybe just wanted to say hello to us, or maybe it was a bit of both—because she began very stiffly to pick her way toward us across the horrible rubble-strewn ground. She stumbled once or twice, and I almost thought she wasn't going to make it, but we kept holding out the food and calling encouragement—"Come on, Daffodil! Good girl, Daffodil!"—and at last she managed to reach us.

She loved all the soft things—the rolls and the crackers and the whole wheat crusts—but the carrots and the apple seemed too hard for her, so we had to bite pieces off and then she was able to take them. Mud couldn't understand why we were giving all the food away! He kept jumping up and trying to snatch some for himself, but we wouldn't let him have it.

"Stop being greedy," I said. "This is a poor little donkey and she needs it."

"It's so cruel, keeping her in all this mess," said Jilly.

"Yes, and she hasn't got any shelter," I said. "What's she supposed to do if it rains?"

There weren't even any trees or bushes. It was really horrible. There was one patch where it looked as if someone had emptied oil out of a car, all black and sticky. And all she had to drink from was an old metal tub with green slime running down the sides.

"I don't think it's right," I said.

"No, and her feet are funny," said Jilly. "Look! They're all big and clumpy."

"Like fuzzy slippers."

"Yes, or clogs."

Her front hooves were all splayed out and turned up at the ends. I'd never seen a donkey with feet like that, but then I really hadn't seen that many donkeys. For all I knew, it was natural. All the same, I didn't think she ought to be kept by herself in that scrubby bit of field without any shelter, and littered with old car parts. Some of them must have been there for ages, because they were half-embedded in the ground and starting to get rusty. It wasn't surprising that poor Daffodil found it difficult to walk. She could hardly move without stepping on something sharp.

We kissed her and whispered that we would be back the next day with more food, but I really hated to leave her like that. She looked so forlorn, standing there with her head down.

When we got home I tried talking to Mom about her, but Mom was tired—she had actually been doing some *ironing*! A huge pile of it—and all she wanted to do was put her feet up and watch television. When I told her about Daffodil she sighed and said, "If there's water there, then someone's obviously looking after her."

"But she doesn't have any shelter!" I said. "And the place is *foul*."

"I agree it wasn't very nice," said Mom. "But I don't expect she's fussy."

"But suppose it rains? Then what does she do?"

"She dries out again!" snapped Mom. "Don't worry about her. I'm sure that donkeys are very hardy."

I told Mom that most donkeys might be hardy, but that I didn't think Daffodil was.

"She couldn't chew the carrots, and her legs are all stiff."

"So she's probably old. It happens to all of us! Anyway, she's all right for the moment because the weather's nice and warm and she's all filled up with rolls and good whole wheat bread. What more could a donkey ask?"

"Companionship," I thought. "And lovely soft grass. And a little shelter filled with hay."

"Clara, I'm glad that you care," said Mom, "but you must guard against becoming obsessed."

"How can I help it?" I cried. "When there's so much cruelty going on?"

"You can only do what you can do," said Mom.

"Well," I said, "Jilly and I have sworn to do as much as we possibly can." I told Mom that it had become our mission in life. "Now that we are Animal Lovers."

Mom said, "Just so long as your schoolwork doesn't suffer."

When I met Jilly the next morning for school, she was looking really down.

"My mom's been on my back," she said.

"Why?" I asked. "What have you done? We got home by 4:30!"

"I know, but I asked her if I could take $5 out of the bank and she said what for, and I told her

35

what it was for, and she said she wasn't sure she wanted me mixed up in that sort of thing."

"What sort of thing?"

"Animal Lovers."

"Why not?"

"I dunno. She seems to think they might go around smashing windows, or something."

"Well, they don't," I said. " 'Cause it says on their leaflet, *strictly peaceful.*"

"I know. I told her. She still doesn't like it."

"She's batty," I said.

"She's my mom," said Jilly.

"She's not going to stop you from joining?" I asked anxiously.

"No, but she says my schoolwork's got to come first."

"Oh, well! Mine says *that*," I said.

That afternoon, when we got back from school, we didn't bother with dinner but collected some more food and went off immediately with Mud to see Daffodil again. This time she really did recognize us! She was standing by the shabby old fence with her head hanging over the edge, desperately trying to reach some of the juicy grass that grew there. When we called out to her she looked up and made this funny braying sound.

"Ee-aw!"

Donkeys really *do* say ee-aw! It suddenly made me realize why the donkey in *Winnie-the-Pooh* is called Eeyore. It had never struck me before, but that's because I read the book when I was only about six and didn't have much in the way of brains.

Daffodil was really happy to see us. She munched up the food we had brought her—more rolls and bread—and let us stroke her and pet her as if she were a dog. But all around her was this terrible mess of old car parts, and I just couldn't bear it. I said to Jilly, "I'm going to go in there and clear some of it away."

Daffodil didn't bat an eye when I scrambled over the fence and dropped into the field beside her. Mud did, of course! He barked, loudly, and began jumping up and down in a frenzy. He hates anyone going somewhere he can't. Daffodil seemed a bit alarmed at the racket he was making; she pulled her ears back and rolled her eyes, and I had to go and comfort her until in the end Mud shut up.

I managed to pick up some of the trash and chuck it inside the burned-out car, but there was just too much of it, and Jilly was starting to nag at me.

"Come *on*, Clara!"

Our moms had made this rule, home by 4:30, and it was nearly that already. I kept saying, "I'll just do a bit more! I'll just do that bit over there," because I really did want Daffodil to have at least a small patch of ground where she could walk without hurting herself. In the end Jilly had to threaten me that she'd take Mud and go back without me if I didn't come *immediately*.

"Oh, all right," I said. Reluctantly, I clambered back over the fence. "At least it's a little bit better," I said. "But we'll have to come again and finish it."

All Jilly could say was, "Quick, or my mom will be furious!"

"When we come tomorrow," I said as I huffed and puffed across the fields behind a galloping Jilly, "I think we ought to bring a piece of rope with us." That way, we could tie Mud to the branch of a tree and could both go into the field and clear junk. "And then," I said, "if we could find some hay from somewhere . . ."

I had visions that by the end of the week all the disgusting trash would be stashed out of sight inside the car and Daffodil would be knee-deep in a bed of beautiful, sweet-smelling hay, or maybe straw. I was so ignorant I didn't know what the difference was! I do now. Hay is dried grass; straw is the stalks of corn or barley. But at the time I thought they were the same thing, and I didn't have any idea where you got them from, even. A pet shop, maybe. But we didn't have a pet shop in Riddlestone, so I would have to get it on Saturday when we went into town with Mom.

"I wonder," I panted as I raced after Jilly, "how much it costs to buy hay?"

Jilly didn't bother to reply, or more probably she didn't have any breath left. She was going like the wind, with Mud cantering joyously at her side. He loves anything that seems like a chase.

"It can't be that much," I said, "can it?"

I thought that I would raid Julius Caesar again. I still had about $3 in there; surely you could buy quite a lot of hay for $3? Enough to keep a little donkey happy? And in the meantime we would clear out the field and make it ready. Tomorrow we would get rid of the trash, and Thursday we would clean out the water tub, and Friday . . .

Friday, I thought, we would borrow Mom's garden shears and cut loads and loads of juicy grass to scatter around until we could put the hay down. Or the straw. Whichever was the cheapest.

I tried to tell Jilly all the things that we were going to do, but I don't think she heard me, or if she did, she didn't take any notice. She was too busy galloping. And as it happened, we weren't able to do any of them anyway.

When we met for school the next morning, we were both looking glum.

"My mom was so mad at me last night," said

Jilly. "She said if I couldn't be trusted to get home when I'd promised to get home then she wasn't going to let me go anymore. It was your fault," she added. "You *wouldn't* come when I told you. And now you'll get to go by yourself"—her voice rose to a self-pitying wail—"and Daffodil will forget all about me!"

"She'll forget all about both of us," I muttered.

"Why?" Jilly looked at me. Sort of—hopefully, almost. "Was your mom mad too?"

"She was furious."

I'd explained to Mom why I was late. I'd told her about clearing the trash. All she said was, "I'm sorry, Clara. You've let me down. I don't want you going across those fields after school anymore. In the summer, maybe, but not at this time of year."

I'd pleaded and begged and said that I was sorry about five million times, but she wouldn't budge.

"I know it was my fault," I said humbly to Jilly. "But I really did want to make things nice for Daffodil!"

Chapter 4

Sometimes it seems that you are just in trouble all the way around. It is not easy trying to help animals when everyone is against you. First it was our moms, being mad at us for being late, showing that they cared more about our dinner getting cold than about a poor neglected donkey having to live in a garbage dump. Next it was Miss Milsom, our class teacher, at the start of the morning recess, asking could we stay behind, please, as she wanted a word with us.

All the rest of the class went trooping off to enjoy themselves, leaving Jilly and me to our fate. Being kept behind by Miss Milsom is *no joke*. Mercy Humphries rolled her eyes at us as she went past, and one or two of the others made sympathetic faces, but Geraldine Hooper just smiled a superior smile and old No-Neck did this sly smirk. They'd be really pleased if we got told off.

Not that I could think of anything we'd done that deserved being told off. At the beginning of the semester, when we'd had our crush on Erik the Gorgeous, we'd been a bit wild and had gone dashing over to the senior wing about twenty times a day, hiding ourselves in closets in the hope of spying him through the keyhole, but ever since rescuing Mud we'd been too involved in the animal thing to mess around like that. But, of course, you never know what a teacher is going to pick on.

I couldn't believe it when Miss Milsom said there'd been a complaint about our anti-fur petition! I mean, my eyes just went like saucers. Who would ever complain about someone just trying to stop people from wearing fur coats that had been ripped off the backs of animals?

Geraldine Hooper's mom, that's who. Geraldine Hooper—wouldn't you know it?—had gone running home carrying on about what we were doing, and her mom had gotten into a fury and come raging into school to complain.

"But what about?" asked Jilly. "All we're doing is just asking people to stop gassing poor little minks to death!"

"Yes, and to stop catching poor arctic foxes in horrible bear traps," I added, feeling that I ought to back Jilly up.

"That's all we're doing," said Jilly.

"It's because we can't stand cruelty," I said.

Miss Milsom said she appreciated that, and fighting cruelty was a very commendable thing, but it just so happened that Geraldine Hooper's uncle owned a fur shop (*ugh!*) and had recently had all his windows smashed by animal-rights fanatics.

"So you can understand that her mom is feeling a bit sensitive about it."

I thought that probably the minks and the foxes felt a bit sensitive about it as well, when they had their beautiful fur coats stripped off them, but I didn't dare say so.

"It's not that you've done anything wrong," said Miss Milsom. "It's just that animal rights is an extremely controversial issue."

I frowned. What did she mean, *controversial*?

"Not everyone looks at things the way you do," said Miss Milsom.

There was a pause, then Jilly found her tongue.

"You mean, there are people who think it's *all right* to gas animals to death?"

"Well, it's difficult, you see," said Miss Milsom. "If it's animals like minks. It's not as if it's breaking any law."

"But it's torture!" said Jilly.

Jilly can be so bold. I wouldn't have the courage to talk back to Miss Milsom like that! I am bold when it comes to action, Jilly is bold when it comes to argument. I expect that is why we are best friends.

Unfortunately, Miss Milsom remained totally unmoved, because all she said was that "torture is a very colored word." She then went on to tell us that in the future we weren't to bring any petitions into school without asking her first.

"I know how committed you both are, but you must understand that to some people it's not so black and white."

45

She smiled at us quite nicely, but Jilly and I felt utterly dejected.

"It *is* black and white," said Jilly as we went out onto the playground. "Cruelty is cruelty and that's all there is to it!"

I thought at least it must be a bit of a comfort to her to know that she wasn't the only one with a mom who was unsympathetic (even if the other one *was* Geraldine Hooper's), but when I pointed this out to her, Jilly just hunched a shoulder and said gloomily that the more unsympathetic people there were, the harder it was going to be to put an end to animal cruelty. Since this was undoubtedly true, I spent the rest of the day feeling totally depressed.

"And we're not even allowed to go and see Daffodil," moaned Jilly.

"No." I heaved a sigh. "The whole world is against us."

Just because we weren't allowed to visit Daffodil didn't mean we weren't thinking of her. I thought of her all through geography and all through math, and on the way home I told Jilly about my plans for clearing out her field and buying some hay (or straw) to make things more comfortable for her. Jilly cheered up quite a bit when she heard this. She agreed with me that it was something positive we could do.

"I just wish we could do it immediately!"

"I know," I said. "It seems like ages to wait."

"Saturday! That's like forever."

"Especially for a poor little donkey. She'll think we've forgotten all about her."

It was a pity that neither of our moms was going into town before then, but they both have to work during the week. My mom works at home and Jilly's mom works in the local antique shop, so Saturday is the only day, usually, that we ever get to go there.

"I'll ask Mom if we can go in *really early*," I said.

"Like in the morning," urged Jilly.

Mom was quite surprised when I told her I thought it would be a good idea if we got up really early on Saturday.

"Can we, Mom?"

"Well!" she said, and she laughed. "If you think you're capable of it."

I wouldn't be normally, not unless Mom came and shook me, but that Saturday I was wide awake at 6:00, and it was me that had to go and shake Mom.

"My goodness! What's all the big rush?" she asked.

I told her that Jilly and I wanted to go to the pet shop, and she said, "Not *more* toys for Mud? That dog is spoiled rotten!"

Mud has a toy box all his own! In it there are balls and ropes and squeaky toys, and nylon bones and leathery chews and a rubber ring that he likes you to pull. I figured he would love a whole lot more! But I told Mom it wasn't toys for Mud, it was hay for Daffodil.

She just shook her head and said, "You'll never get your new sneakers at this rate."

She just can't accept that now that we are Animal Lovers things like new sneakers are simply of *no importance* in our lives.

As soon as we hit town we left Mom and Benjy to go shopping at the supermarket while we headed off for the pet shop.

Jilly's mom hadn't let her take any money

out of the bank to join Animal Lovers. She'd said that she would lend it to her and that Jilly could pay her back out of her pocket money, which meant she couldn't contribute anything to Daffodil's hay (except that it turned out to be straw because it's cheaper). Jilly was really worried about this, but I said it didn't matter. What bothered me more was how we were going to get the bale of straw back to the car. A bale of straw is quite large and unwieldy. It is also *heavy*. Being townies, we hadn't realized.

Fortunately, the man in the pet shop is really nice. He said that he would put it on his cart for us and we could wheel it all the way to the parking lot. So we asked him if he would keep it for us until we came back, and we went rushing off to the coffee shop where we had said we would meet Mom and Benjy.

"Mom!" I cried. "Mom!"

"Don't tell me," said Mom. "What have you done now?"

"We've bought a bale of straw, Mom! For Daffodil! The pet shop man is going to let us borrow his cart so we can wheel it to the car."

"I see," said Mom. "And then what's going to happen?"

"We're going to take it and put it in Daffodil's field," I said.

"And have you thought how you're going to get it home?"

"Well—in the car," I said.

Mom looked at me. She raised an eyebrow. And suddenly I saw what she meant! Our car is not a hatchback and it only has two doors. It is *tiny*.

"Maybe Clara and I could sit on it?" said Jilly.

"You'll have to," said Mom.

It's a good thing Mom isn't fussy! The inside of the car looked like a farmyard by the time we'd shoved and heaved at the bale of straw and crammed it onto the backseat. There wasn't room for me and Jilly to sit on top of it, and we couldn't ask Benjy to change places because he gets really carsick in the back, even worse than he does in the front, and that is bad enough, believe me. We'd have been stopping every few minutes to let him throw up. So what we had to do was squeeze together at the side, with me squashed onto Jilly's lap.

Jilly complained like mad! First she complained that I was too heavy, then she complained that I was crushing her, and then she complained that my backside was bony. What nerve! I told her to shut up and think of Daffodil.

We decided that when we went to visit Daffodil that afternoon with Mom and Benjy—Benjy *insisted* on coming—we would take Mom's broom and some cleaning supplies and get the place ready for putting down the straw on Sunday.

Mom said, "You're crazy, the two of you!" but I don't think she really thought we were. Or if she did, she didn't mind. She told us we could put the straw in the shed, and she let us borrow her broom and some rubber gloves and a scrubbing brush. She carried the broom while I carried the bucket with all the cleaning stuff inside it, and Jilly carried another couple of buckets that her mom had said she could take "so long as you bring them back in the state in which you found them." We reckoned that we'd need three to hold the water that we were emptying out of Daffodil's old dirty tub.

We also remembered to take a bag full of food. We had:

whole wheat crackers

carrots, cut into small pieces

1 apple, also cut into pieces

3 whole wheat rolls

1 lump of sugar.

I wasn't sure that sugar was good for donkeys because, if it rots human teeth, then surely it must rot donkey teeth as well? But Benjy had really wanted to bring it. He'd been going on all morning about "Dooga lum for Daddledill" (which made Jilly giggle), and I didn't have the heart to say he couldn't. He wanted to give it to her himself, and I thought he ought to be encouraged so that when he grew old enough he might become an Animal Lover like Jilly and me.

"I will feel extremely foolish," said Mom as we trudged across the fields with all our bits and pieces, "if the owner is there."

"I won't," I said. "I'll ask him why he doesn't

look after his donkey properly."

"Not in those tones, I hope," said Mom.

Jilly and I looked at each other and made faces. We'd already discussed what we would do and say if we ever came across Daffodil's owner.

"Excuse *me*," Jilly was going to say. "Is this your donkey?"

And if he said yes (we felt sure it would be a man), we were going to give him a long lecture about how cruel it was to keep one little donkey all on its own without any shelter.

"You'll find a bit of politeness goes a long way," said Mom.

But why should we be polite to a creep who kept his donkey the way that poor Daffodil was kept?

We reached the top of the Down and set off along the path that led to the scrubby patch where Daffodil lived out her lonely existence. She was looking sadder than ever, standing against the fence in the far corner, her head hanging down. She didn't even look up when we called her.

"I think she must be very old," said Mom.

Jilly and I clambered over the fence and went across with our bag of goodies. Daffodil perked up a bit when we showed her the food, but I thought that Mom was probably right and that she was extremely old. Old and stiff and tired. She needed a bit of comfort in her life.

Benjy was eager to feed her the sugar lump, so Mom lifted him up and put him over the fence and he staggered across, through the rubble, and I showed him how to put the sugar on the palm of his hand and hold it out. Daffodil lipped it off so gently! And she let Benjy stroke her, which made him happy. Mud, on his leash with Mom, watched jealously from the other side of the fence. Mud is very protective of Benjy. I think it is because they are both deaf and Mud has realized this.

After we'd fed Daffodil all the food except the rolls, which we were keeping for a treat at the end, we started the great cleanup. First we tipped over the filthy water tub between us and emptied all the water into our three buckets. Then we put the buckets in a safe place, and while Jilly pulled on Mom's rubber gloves and attacked the tub with Mom's scrubbing brush, I took the broom and began to sweep up all the litter, and lots of droppings that I thought shouldn't just be left to decay. I told Benjy, who had gone back to rejoin Mom and Mud, to make himself useful by plucking as much grass as he could, so that we could make a little nest of it for Daffodil to stand on—or to eat, if she preferred.

Benjy really took his task seriously. By the time Jilly and I had finished, and the water tub was shiny clean and the ground reasonably clear, he had picked enough grass to fill two buckets! We scattered it where Daffodil was standing, and fed her three rolls, and kissed her on the nose and whispered that we would be back again tomorrow "to make a nice warm bed for you."

Mom shook her head and said, "I don't know how you're going to get that huge bale of straw all the way up here. I can't help you tomorrow, I'm afraid. I've got some work to catch up on."

"We'll manage," I said.

Next morning we cycled out to the shelter to collect the petition that we'd left there. It was totally filled in! Denise, who is Meg's assistant, told us that we could always bring more if we wanted. We thought that if everybody was like Meg and Denise—and me and Jilly—there wouldn't be any need to fight against cruelty to animals because there wouldn't be any.

We couldn't stay long at the shelter because of getting back to do our vile homework, but before we left we wandered down to the field to look at the donkeys, Doris and Bert.

"Their feet aren't like fuzzy slippers," I said.

"No," agreed Jilly, "but maybe they're a different sort of breed."

Too late, we realized that we should have gotten a donkey book out of the library while we were in town on Saturday morning. We thought of going back to ask Meg or Denise, but when we put our heads around the gate, we saw that the yard was full of people, all wanting to look at the animals and hopefully adopt some, and it didn't seem quite the right moment. It would be just too awful if us interrupting was the cause of someone having second thoughts and going away again.

"In any case, it's the sort of thing we really ought to be able to find out for ourselves," said Jilly.

I agreed that it was, and we decided that what we would do was go to the school library on Monday and see if they had anything about donkeys.

We cycled back home, having agreed to meet again later to take Mud for his walk and drag the bale of straw to Daffy Down. Mom was really helpful. She found a ball of garden twine and wound it all around so that we wouldn't lose too much straw on the way, and then she made two loops out of old belts so that we could both pull together.

It was still a struggle to get it up there! It took us forever, because we kept having to stop and rest, and Mud didn't help. At one point he tried to lift his leg against it! Jilly screamed, and he capered away with such a wicked glint in his eye, so I knew that he had just done it to be naughty. He has a terrific sense of humor, Mud does. He's always doing things to get you going.

"But we don't want it made wet," said Jilly, sternly.

Daffodil was standing in the middle of her little patch. Her head was down again and she didn't look up when we called her, but at least her ears twitched, which seemed like a sign of recognition. We had noticed with Doris and Bert that their heads were always up and alert, but we thought probably they had more to interest them than poor Daffodil. There's always something going on at the shelter, and also they had each other and the old horse, Captain. There were also a couple of goats, so that life was never boring.

We tied Mud to a nearby tree (which he did not like at *all*), then hoisted our bale over the fence and clambered after it. Mom had lent us her kitchen scissors to cut the twine, and we made a nice thick bed of straw all around where Daffodil was standing. She looked at it as if she couldn't believe her eyes!

"I bet she's never seen any before," I said.

We know now that just scattering straw around like that is stupid and wasteful, because it will only get trampled underfoot and mashed into the ground. Then of course if it rains it will get soaking wet and will probably rot, so in fact it wasn't a very sensible thing to do. If we had gotten our donkey book from the library we would have realized this. But at least for a short time Daffodil had a bit of luxury, so we did do *some* good.

After we'd spread the straw, we fed her with some bran crackers that Mrs. Cherry had given us. We'd met her in the lane that morning and told her we were going to feed a donkey, and she'd said, "I've got just the thing," and produced this box of crackers.

"Horrible things," she said. "I got them for the bran, but I can't cope."

Daffodil really enjoyed them!

"I feel a bit better about her now," I said as we went back home with Mud. "At least we know she's got somewhere soft if she wants to lie down."

"Yes, and tomorrow we'll go to the school library," said Jilly, "and get out a book about donkeys."

Chapter 5

Would you believe it? There wasn't one single book about donkeys in our school library! Mrs. Jenkins looked it up on the computer and was very apologetic.

"But if you want to find out about donkeys there's a wonderful place called the Donkey Sanctuary somewhere down in Devon."

Devon! But that is so far away.

"Now what do we do?" wailed Jilly as we trailed off to math class. "We can't go all the way to Devon!"

I pulled myself together. One of us had to have a bit of backbone.

"Next time we go into town," I said, "we'll go to the library and find out the address. Then we can write and ask them to send us some information."

"So long as they don't want money," said Jilly, " 'cause my mom won't let me take any more from the bank. She says I've got to save it."

Yes, and Julius Caesar was almost empty.

"At least we can find out," I said.

That evening when I was trying to do my homework, Mud made the biggest nuisance of himself. It was math, which I can never do anyway. He really got on my nerves. He kept jumping up and batting at me, and once he stretched out a paw and pulled everything off the table. I yelled at him—"*Mud!* Stop that!"— but he's not used to me being mad at him, and I guess he thought it was all part of the game because two minutes later he actually jumped right onto the table and trampled on my math book, scrunching all the pages and even tearing a big hole in one of them. I screamed, and walloped him, and he went scooting out into the hall with his ears pulled back.

"You stupid dog!" I yelled. I gathered all my things together and stormed into the kitchen, where Mom was sitting at the table writing something.

"Now what's the matter?" asked Mom.

"I can't do my math," I told her.

Mom sighed. "Why not?"

"I can't understand it! It doesn't make any sense."

Figures never make very much sense to me; I like words a whole lot better. And pictures better still! Usually, Mom would have told me to sit down and we'd have worked through it together. And she'd have explained what it all meant and gone over it about ten times until I had it firmly fixed in my head (I am really *dumb* when it comes to math), but today she just said rather impatiently, "I can't help you, Clara. I'm sorry. I'm far too busy. You'll have to make a bit of an effort to try to work it out for yourself."

"I've tried! I can't!"

"In that case, tell your teacher. Ask him to go through it with you. That's what he's there for."

"But he went through it already! In class. I'm supposed to know how to do it!"

"Look," said Mom, "just stop panicking. Think about it calmly. There's no mystery attached; it's all perfectly logical."

She obviously wasn't going to help me, and Mr. Timbrell was going to be furious and accuse me of not paying attention. (Which actually I hadn't been. I'd been thinking about Daffodil and wondering how we could make a little shelter for her.)

"I'm going to go next door," I said, "and ask Jilly."

Jilly is like some kind of mathematical genius. She would do it for me.

It was Jilly's mom who let me in. She is very small and neat and pretty, but she has a sort of pinched look about her.

"Oh, Clara," she said. "Come in. If you want Jilly to help walk the dog, I'm afraid it's far too late and anyway she's doing her homework."

I said that Mud had already been for his walk and that I just wanted to ask Jilly something. "If that's all right."

"Well, be quick," said Mrs. Montague. "She's out in the back."

When Jilly's mom said "the back," she meant the kitchen. Mrs. Montague's kitchen is sparkling and neat as a pin, and Jilly always does her homework out there. Except that when I opened the door she wasn't doing homework but standing on the counter, flapping at the window with a towel.

"What *are* you up to?" I asked.

"I'm trying to catch a fly," said Jilly, and she dabbed again and cried, "Got it!" and jumped down off the counter and raced for the back door. "I've rescued three already," she said proudly.

Well, I suppose it is more fun than doing math homework.

"I think actually they were dying," said Jilly. "I think that's what they do when the weather gets cold. But at least it's better if they die outside than get stuck up on Mom's fly-trap thing. I hate seeing their poor corpses."

"Mud gobbles all ours," I said. "He just jumps up and snaps at them."

"Well, a dog has to eat," said Jilly. "I mean, it's nature, isn't it? What are you doing here, anyway?"

Instead of saying that I wanted her to help me with my math, I suddenly blurted out, "I walloped him!"

"Who?" asked Jilly.

"Mud. I walloped him!" I hadn't realized until that moment how bad I felt about it. He was only a poor little deaf dog, trying to be helpful.

Jilly was looking at me as if I were a mass murderer.

"What did you wallop him for?"

"Because he kept pawing at me when I was trying to do my math homework!"

"You walloped him just for that?"

"Yes, because I can't do it and Mr. Timbrell's going to be mad at me and Mom won't help me, so please will you?"

"Well, I will," said Jilly, "so long as you promise as soon as you go back you'll make it up to Mud. I never heard of anything so mean! Walloping a poor little deaf dog just for being affectionate."

I giggled. "He wasn't being affectionate, he was being naughty!"

"I wouldn't wallop him for being naughty," said Jilly. "I'd like it if he was naughty. It's so unfair!" she said. "I helped rescue him and now I hardly ever see him!"

"It's not my fault," I said. "If your mom would let him come in here, he could live half the time with you and half the time with me." But even as I said it, I knew that I couldn't bear not to have Mud with me the whole time. Mom even lets him sleep on my bed at night, and he cuddles with me and makes these little whiffling noises. I felt desperately sorry for Jilly, because I know that she loves Mud just as much as I do.

"Maybe one day your mom will change her mind," I said.

"Pigs might fly!" said Jilly.

We agreed that when we were grown up we would live together in a trailer in the middle of a field, surrounded by dogs and cats, donkeys and horses, geese and chickens, and every sort of animal you could think of.

"And we won't ever get married or have children," said Jilly.

"No," I agreed, "because husbands and children are such a nuisance."

"There'll just be us and the animals."

"Yes, and they'll all be rescued, and now, *please*," I said, "*please* could you help me with my math?"

Jilly said that I could copy hers but that I had better put a few mistakes in, or Mr. Timbrell would be suspicious.

I apologized like crazy to Mud when I got back, but he is such a sweet-natured dog! He doesn't ever hold grudges. We slept together the same as usual and he whiffled contentedly the whole night through.

Toward the middle of the week the weather grew colder, and Jilly and I worried about Daffodil, alone in her field without any shelter.

"I'm going to go and see her!" I said.

"How can you?" wailed Jilly. "We're not allowed during the week!"

"I don't care. I'm going to!"

That night I raided the food closet and helped myself to some bread and crackers and put them in a plastic container in my school bag, and Thursday morning, when Jilly and I met for school, I said, "I'm going up there."

"*Now?*" shrieked Jilly. "You'll miss attendance! Miss Milsom'll be really mad!"

"But Daffodil could be starving to death!" I said.

Jilly thought about it and said why didn't I go during the lunch recess?

"There'd be less chance of being found out. Of course, it'd mean missing lunch . . ."

I didn't mind about lunch, just so long as I could get to see Daffodil.

"I'll buy you a bag of chips," promised Jilly.

As soon as the 1:00 bell rang, I went running out of school and up to the Down just as fast as my legs would carry me. I knew I was taking a big risk, because skipping school is one of the things that makes adults really mad, but it was worth it. Daffodil was so pleased to see me! She whinnied and brayed, and made her funny ee-aw noise and nuzzled with her nose in my hand.

I was sad to see that most of our nice clean straw had been trampled into the mud or blown around by the wind, and I thought that probably what we should have done was to buy hay and put it in a net so that Daffodil could eat it. I said this to Jilly when I arrived back, all pink and panting, at school, and she wisely said that you learn by your mistakes, though I felt it was too bad that we had to learn at the expense of a poor little donkey.

"We should have thought about it," I said.

"Well, but we can't think of everything," said Jilly. "And maybe she ate some of the straw. If donkeys do eat straw," she added.

"You see?" I said. "We don't know *anything*. And she still doesn't have any shelter! She hasn't even got another little donkey to cuddle up to," I said, thinking of how Mud and I cuddled under the comforter. (I didn't say this to Jilly for fear of upsetting her.) "I just don't think it's right!"

Jilly agreed. She said that she didn't think it was right, either.

"But what can we do? We've done all we can!"

I said, "We're supposed to be Animal Lovers! We're supposed to be helping animals!"

That really made Jilly unhappy. I guess she thought I was criticizing her, which perhaps I was, in a way. But I wasn't just criticizing Jilly, I was criticizing both of us.

We bickered and squabbled all the rest of the afternoon, and all the way home. In fact, we almost had a mega fight but just managed not to. It was because we were so worried and felt so helpless, and there just didn't seem to be anyone we could turn to. Also, we both had this sort of feeling that, as Animal Lovers, we ought to be able to solve problems on our own.

All the same, I thought it couldn't hurt just to try asking Mom. Unfortunately, I chose a bad moment. Mom almost bit my head off.

"Clara, do you *have* to keep bothering me about that wretched donkey? Can't you see that I'm busy?"

"You're always busy," I said resentfully.

"Yes!" snapped Mom. "Busy trying to earn enough money to keep body and soul together! Not to mention buying food for that huge dog. *And* feeding other people's donkeys! How much more do you want me to do?"

I wasn't really sure what I did want Mom to do. Just listen to me, maybe. Or maybe I wanted her to take over and say, "Leave it to me. I'll get something done about it." And then she would get in touch with the RSPCA, for example; that's the Royal Society for the Prevention of Cruelty to Animals, like the ASPCA in America, and they would come along and look at Daffodil and say, "Oh, this is not right!" She would be taken away to . . . to the Donkey Sanctuary, and they would look after her for the rest of her days, and I wouldn't have to worry about her anymore.

But just like she wouldn't help me with my math homework, Mom wasn't going to help me with Daffodil, either. If anything was going to be done, then it was up to Jilly and me.

"Just don't keep going on about it," said Mom. "I have a job to finish, and if I don't finish it on time, I'm going to be in trouble. So try to be a little bit less selfish for once in your life and give me a bit of breathing space. All right?"

I tried not to be hurt, because I know Mom

didn't mean it. Saying I was selfish, that is. I *wasn't* being selfish, I was caring about a dumb animal! But it was like when I walloped Mud. I only walloped him because I was bothered about my math homework. Mom only snapped at me because she was bothered about money and about getting her job finished.

What Mom does is she works as a translator. There's this agency in London, and they send her all this stuff that has to be translated from foreign languages into English. I suppose Mom is really smart. She can do French, Spanish, Italian, and *Russian*! Russian is really difficult. They don't even write their letters the same way we do. For instance, this is how they would write my name in Russian:

КЛАРА КАРЭР

I asked Mom once if she knew any swear words in other languages and she said yes, but she wasn't going to teach them to me, which I think is mean!

She doesn't get to translate many swear

words. The work the agency sends her is mostly boring technical stuff, like at the moment she was translating pages and *pages*, practically a whole book, all about aluminum, and that was why she was so mad and crabby. But I understood and so I forgave her. Mud hadn't held any grudges against me and I decided that I wouldn't hold any against Mom. All the same, I did wish there was someone I could talk to.

I could talk to Jilly, of course, but Jilly couldn't do anything any more than I could. We really needed a grown-up.

"Let's see what happens on Saturday," said Jilly.

But Saturday came and we couldn't go into town because of Mom still tearing her hair out over her aluminum. She kept saying there was a deadline and if she didn't meet the deadline the agency would stop giving her work.

I could tell she was feeling a bit guilty because she added that once she had met the deadline she would be able to relax.

"And then I'll talk to you all you like about

your wretched donkey!"

The trouble was, Mom's deadline was days away. Anything could happen to Daffodil between then and now.

"It could pour with rain," I said to Jilly, as we tramped up to Daffy Down on our own, with Mud, that Saturday afternoon.

Jilly sighed. "Maybe donkeys don't mind rain."

It was true that Mud didn't seem to mind it. In fact the wetter—and muddier!—he got, the more frisky it made him. But Mud was always wiped down with his own special dog towel the minute we got home. He probably wouldn't be so happy if he were just left wet and cold, like Daffodil.

We had to clamber into the field again because, however much we called, she wouldn't come to us. We fed her her rolls (which we had had to buy out of my pocket money! Jilly's mom said she didn't have anything and I didn't dare ask mine), and we stroked her and petted her, but she seemed very down. She hardly lifted her head up at all and didn't once make her lovely ee-aw sound.

A few shabby bits of straw were still there, but most of it had been churned up in the mud. There were also lots of droppings all over. I couldn't help wondering if they ought to be there. I'd heard of horse caretakers "mucking out," and I'd always thought what it meant was clearing away all the dirty bedding and putting down fresh hay.

"Except that maybe it doesn't have to be done if they're living outside? Maybe you just leave it to . . . to dry up, or something?"

We just didn't know.

We kicked away some of the muck with our boots, but the field honestly didn't look all that much better than it had right at the beginning. It was really depressing.

"And you spent all that money!" moaned Jilly.

But I didn't care about the money. I just cared about Daffodil.

"We have *got* to find out about donkeys," I said.

The only person we could think of was Meg. We never like to call her, as a rule, unless it's *really* important, because she is one of the busiest and most dedicated people that we know, and it's not right to waste her time with idle chatter. But as Jilly said, "It is about animals."

We heaped up what was left of the straw and kissed Daffodil good-bye, and trudged back down the hill again. As soon as we got home we tried calling the shelter, but as usual the number was busy. We tried and we tried, but we could just never get through. Even when it rang, no one was answering.

It was dark by now so we knew we wouldn't be allowed to get on our bikes and ride out there. Our moms would have a joint fit at the very thought.

"We'll just have to try again in the morning," said Jilly.

So we did, and at long last we got through. It was Denise who answered. She sounded out of breath and flustered.

"Oh! Clara," she said. "What can I do for you? We're up to our eyes! Meg's been out all night rescuing stray cats, we've got an emergency with one of the dogs, and the place is just generally going mad. Is it anything urgent, or can it possibly wait?"

My heart sank right down into my boots.

"It's nothing especially urgent," I said.

Jilly was glaring at me, her eyes like daggers, but when I explained about the stray cats and the doggy emergency, she agreed that it was all I could have said.

"Maybe we should call the RSPCA?" I suggested.

But we couldn't get through to them, either!

It was then that Jilly had what seemed like a really brave and brilliant idea.

"You know what I think we should do? I think we should try to find out who her owner is. It can't be that difficult. It's got to be someone near."

We'd noticed that just down the hill, a short way away from Daffodil's horrible piece of scrubland, there was a small cluster of houses, rather shabby looking, with lots of old broken-down cars and motorcycles scattered around.

"I bet it's someone who lives there," said Jilly. "I think we should go and find them and talk to them."

"When?" I asked.

"Now!" said Jilly. "I think we should go by ourselves in case they have horrible, vicious dogs that don't like Mud, and then we can take Mud for his walk this afternoon same as usual and see Daffodil."

"But what about our homework?" I said.

It is unlike me to be timid where action is concerned, but I was just so surprised by Jilly coming over all masterful like that. I think perhaps she surprised herself.

"Forget homework!" she cried. "Daffodil's more important than homework!"

Chapter 6

We didn't tell our moms what we were going to do because you just never know, with grown-ups, whether they'll find some reason for stopping you. Mom thought I was at Jilly's doing my homework, and Jilly's mom thought that she was with me. We didn't actually say that that was where we were going to be, but it was what they seemed to think.

I said to Jilly, as we raced off down the lane, that if we'd taken Mud with us we wouldn't have needed to deceive them because then we really *could* have done our homework.

"Only this afternoon instead of this morning."

"Yes, but suppose they have vicious dogs?" said Jilly. "They might attack him."

I wasn't sure why Jilly thought that the people

in the houses would have vicious dogs, but she said that anyone who lived in a mess of old car parts and broken-down motorcycles always did.

"They have Rottweilers and Dobermans and they train them to kill. You don't want Mud *killed*, do you?"

Of course I didn't, and so I shut up, and after a few minutes Jilly said, "We'd still be deceiving them, anyway. They still wouldn't know where we were going."

"No, and if they did they'd be bound to find *some* reason to say no."

"They always do," said Jilly.

It was easier to reach the houses by road than going all the way up to Daffy Down, so we didn't see Daffodil that morning. As it happened, we weren't going to see her that afternoon, either, but fortunately we didn't know that at the time.

The houses were in a circle around a shabby bit of grass that had a big notice in the middle saying *No Games*. A woman was walking a dog up and down it, and the dog was—a Rottweiler!

"I told you so," hissed Jilly.

It's funny, but I am not scared of animals. I am scared of lots and lots of things, really silly things sometimes, like making stupid remarks or being laughed at, but animals don't scare me one little bit. I went marching boldly up to the woman, just to show Jilly that there was nothing to be frightened of, and said, "Excuse me, but we're looking for the person who owns the donkey."

The woman jerked a thumb. "That'll be him over there. Number 3."

I thanked her politely and held out my hand to the Rottweiler, who sniffed it cautiously, then wagged his stumpy tail (it had been *docked*) to show that he approved.

"That's a nice dog," I said.

"Old Bruno," said the woman. "My big baby, aren't you?" And then, perhaps because I had spoken nicely to her dog, she added, "Number 3. His name's Grissom. He's a bit of an old so-and-so, but he's harmless."

I thanked her again and ran back to Jilly, who was standing by the *No Games* notice

81

pretending to study it.

"Mr. Grissom," I said. "Number 3." I couldn't believe it had been so easy! "He's a bit of an old so-and-so, but he's harmless."

"I don't call it harmless," said Jilly, "keeping a donkey the way he keeps Daffodil."

This time it was Jilly who went marching off. I trailed behind her, wondering what we were going to say. I thought it would probably be best if I didn't say anything but left it to Jilly. Jilly is good at saying things. I get rather nervous and tongue-tied. I would only mess it up for her.

Jilly strode purposefully in at the gate of number 3 and turned impatiently to wait for me.

"Are you coming?"

"Yes!" I hurried after her, up the garden path. The front yard of number 3 was dismal, just old cracked concrete with a few straggly weeds that had managed to break through here and there. There were old oil drums stacked in one corner and a motorcycle with only one wheel propped against the wall of the house, beneath the front window. I thought that if this was how Mr. Grissom lived he probably didn't see anything wrong with the way he kept Daffodil.

Jilly punched her finger at the doorbell.

"What did you say his name was? Gristle?"

"Grissom." I giggled nervously.

"There's nothing *funny*," said Jilly.

"N-no," I said, and I hiccuped.

"Oh, Clara, honestly!"

"I c-can't help it—hic! It just—hic!—happens."

"Well, do something to stop it happening," said Jilly. "Hold your breath or stand on your head or something."

I thought that I would definitely leave all the talking to her.

After what seemed like hours, the front door opened and we saw this old man standing there. He was bald and shriveled and looked like a gnome. And he didn't have any teeth! Just a piece of one, right in the middle, all yellow and pointy. I'd never seen anybody without any teeth before. Just gums. It was really horrible.

I would never have known what to say if Jilly hadn't been there but Jilly can always think of something. She said, "Good morning, Mr.

Gristle, I mean Grissom. Excuse us for bothering you, but we've come about your donkey."

"Is that a fact?" said Mr. Grissom.

"It is your donkey up there, isn't it?"

"Might be," said Mr. Grissom. "Might not be. All depends, don't it?"

There was a pause. I could tell that even Jilly for once was at a bit of a loss. I was racking my brain how to help her when Mr. Grissom said, "What you want to know for?"

"Well . . ." Jilly took a breath. I wondered what had happened to the lecture she had been going to give him. "We were a bit worried about her," she said.

"Worried? About that old donkey? You got no cause to worry about that old donkey!"

"*Is* she old?" I asked.

"Must be all of 19 or 20. Used to belong to my son, see. Had her for years. Then he goes off, and I get the job. I go up and check her out every so often, make sure she's still there. Fill the dratted water tub. Give her a bite to eat. It's not everyone'd do that. There's some that just keeps 'em on grass."

"But there isn't any grass there," said Jilly. "Well, hardly any."

"Enough for her. She has it easy! Never done what I'd call a real day's work in her life. Not like some of 'em, poor little devils, hefting big heavy loads up and down."

"She must get lonely, though," said Jilly. "All by herself."

"Lonely? Don't you believe it! Put another donkey in there, she'd give it a real tough time. Resent it, she would, after all these years."

Jilly swallowed. Rather timidly I said, "We thought her feet looked a bit peculiar."

"Peculiar? In what way?"

"Sort of . . . turned up," I said. "Like a fuzzy slipper."

"Natural, that is. It's the hooves growing. On account she don't do no work, but just stands around all day. They don't get ground down, see? Stands to reason, if you think about it."

"But doesn't it hurt her?" I asked.

"Lord bless you, no! You'll find it in lots of old donkeys. That answered all your questions? Or you got some more? Go on! You go ahead!

You ask me whatever you like."

"We did just wonder," said Jilly, "what happens in the winter? I mean . . . shouldn't she have some kind of shelter?"

"Shelter? Donkeys don't need shelter! Got fur coats, haven't they? What they need shelter for? Not pampered creatures like your racehorses. Hardy little devils donkeys are. Don't you worry your pretty little heads about that old mule! There's plenty worse off than her. Tough old bird, that one."

"Is it all right if we feed her?" asked Jilly.

"You feed her as much as you like!" Mr. Grissom gave a throaty chuckle. We could hear it crackling and bubbling all the way down inside him. "I've no objections to you feeding her. Means I can cut down on the food bill!"

"We're only giving her *good* things," I said earnestly. "Carrots and apples and whole wheat bread."

"That's the ticket! You spoil her. I noticed someone had put some straw in there. Bit of a waste, but there you go. If that's what you want to spend your money on."

"We just wanted to make it comfortable for her," I said.

"I'll tell you what, little girls." Mr. Grissom leaned toward us. Jilly stood her ground, but I took a step backward. "Donkeys is only animals. Right? Only animals. You remember that."

"What a horrible old man," said Jilly as we walked back down the road.

"Yes, but at least he told us some things we didn't know. Like about the feet, and donkeys being hardy. And the fact that she's old."

Twenty years sounded really ancient. I knew that dogs hardly ever live that long and so I thought it must be the same for donkeys.

"Poor Daffodil!" I said. "She's such an old person."

It was only later we discovered that in fact donkeys can live to be as old as 40, or even 45, so that in donkey terms Daffodil was really only middle-aged.

Lots of things that Mr. Grissom told us weren't true—Meg said later that he had "deceived us"—but we couldn't have known. We'd done our best and were quite pleased and proud of ourselves.

"That's what it's all about," said Jilly, "being an Animal Lover. It means you have to go and investigate and talk to people and make sure that their animals are being properly looked after."

We both agreed that although Mr. Grissom was horrible, he had at least set our minds at rest. We still felt sad about Daffodil, because she was so old and probably wouldn't live much longer, but we could stop worrying about her strange turned-up feed and her stiff legs and the fact that she didn't have any shelter. She didn't need any shelter. Donkeys were hardy. Mr. Grissom had said so.

I was so relieved about all this that I made the mistake of telling Mom. I thought she'd be happy, because now I would stop nagging her, but instead she went into the most terrible rage and said, "So that's where you've been! You told me you were going to Jilly's!"

I protested that I hadn't ever actually said that I was going to Jilly's, but Mom snapped that I had "deliberately given her that impression." It turned out that Jilly's dad had telephoned all the way from America, and her mom had come around to find her and discovered that she wasn't here. So then Mom had said, "I thought they were both with you," and Jilly's mom had said, "No, I thought they were with you." Then they had both gotten really angry and couldn't wait for us to get back so they could yell at us.

Mom said it was the underhanded way I'd behaved that made her so angry, but she also said that I was "old enough to know better than to go wandering off to speak to strange men."

"But there were two of us," I said, "and we *had* to find out about Daffodil. You were right, Mom!" (I said this in the hope of making her less angry.) "She *is* old. She's 20. And donkeys don't need shelter because they're hardy, but we can go on feeding her, and—"

"Not today, you can't! For the rest of the day, my girl, you're going to stay indoors and do your homework."

"But, Mom! Mud hasn't been for his walk!"

"Whose fault is that?" said Mom. "He'll just have to go without a walk for today."

It's so unfair, taking it out on a poor little dog!

On Monday my beautiful badge came from the Animal Lovers. It's bright buttercup yellow with these two little pictures of a cat and a dog, and around the edge it says WE LOVE ANIMALS in big writing. I was really excited by it and wanted to wear it immediately, but I'd promised Jilly, and so I couldn't. They'd also sent me a copy of the Junior Newsletter and I couldn't read that, either, because Jilly had begged me.

"*Please* don't look at it before I get mine!"

So what I did was I took it in to school with me and we read it together during recess. Jilly was really grateful! She said that not many people would have done that.

"But we're friends," I said.

Jilly said yes, but that didn't always mean anything. She said, "I had this friend in elementary school once. She promised me *faithfully* she'd let me have first try on her new bike, and then she went and let someone else and pretended she'd never promised, which she *had*, so after that we weren't friends anymore."

"We'll always be friends," I said, "because of the animals."

Chapter 7

Next day was Saturday, and for the second week running we couldn't go into town. Mom was still fretting over her deadline and Jilly's mom was at the shop, so there we were, stuck. I tried suggesting to Mom that maybe Jilly and I could catch a bus and go in by ourselves, but she seemed convinced we would do something stupid like get lost or go off with strangers.

"I'm not sure how much I can trust you anymore."

"Mom!" I cried. "That was for *Daffodil!*"

"This animal thing is getting out of hand," said Mom. "What do you want to go into town for, anyway?"

I said to get out a book about donkeys and

find out about the Donkey Sanctuary, and borrow another wildlife video (or one about donkeys).

"You see what I mean?" cried Mom. "*Animals!* You'll become an animal bore if you're not careful."

It is lovely in many ways to live in the country, but the great drawback is when you are stranded there and cannot get out. For once I felt totally down and dejected and it was Jilly who had to talk me out of it.

"Look," she said, "if we did our homework this morning, it would give us all of tomorrow for walking Mud and visiting Daffodil. We could even go down to the animal shelter."

"Yes." I brightened slightly. Before we'd had Mud, we used to go to the shelter almost every day and help with the animals, but now that we had him to look after we couldn't always manage it. It made me feel a bit guilty sometimes.

"We could spend all tomorrow morning there," said Jilly.

"Yes, we could," I said, and I didn't feel anywhere near as down as I had before. Sometimes you need a friend to cheer you up.

Unfortunately things didn't quite work out the way we had planned. In fact, we didn't get to the shelter all that weekend.

It was absolutely freezing when we took Mud for his walk on Saturday afternoon. The wind was roaring and howling across the fields and up on the Down it was so strong we could hardly walk against it. Just to make matters worse it had started to rain, big icy splatters that stung your cheeks and made your eyes water. Even Mud became a bit subdued. As for poor Daffodil, she was a pitiful sight, huddled by the fence with her head hanging down.

"Oh!" cried Jilly. "I just don't *believe* she doesn't need a shelter!"

I didn't believe it, either.

"We've got to do something!" I said.

"But what? It's no good asking that horrible old man! He won't do anything."

"No. We've got to. It's up to us."

We fed Daffodil the food we had brought her, but she needed a lot of coaxing. It was almost as if she had just given up and decided that life wasn't worth living anymore. All that remained of her nice warm bed of straw was a mud-caked mess.

"I wish we could take her home with us," said Jilly.

We couldn't do that, but I suddenly thought of something that we *could* do.

"We could make her a coat! A waterproof coat!"

Jilly looked at me doubtfully. "How?"

"We could get a blanket and . . . fold it in half and . . . and put some plastic garbage bags over it!"

"Mm," said Jilly. She still sounded doubtful. I felt quite impatient with her for not being more enthusiastic. Why was she so weak? All I wanted to do was race back home and get started! All Jilly could think to do was whine.

"Where would we get a blanket from?"

"Anywhere! Off a bed."

"We don't have blankets on our beds."

Neither did we.

"I know!" I said. "Mom's got a big thick car rug. We could use that."

"Would she let us?"

"We don't have to *tell* her," I said. "We're only going to borrow it."

"But won't she be mad? If it gets messed up?"

I was really disappointed in Jilly. Calling herself an Animal Lover and worrying in case Mom—my mom!—got mad about her rug being messed up.

"This could be saving an animal's life," I said.

So then she shut up and didn't say any more, but I'd obviously jolted her out of her wimpishness because she agreed to come around after dinner and help me. And when she came she actually brought two very large green plastic bags that her mom used for garden waste.

"They're better than ordinary garbage bags. They don't break as easily."

I asked Mom if I could borrow the sewing basket. Mom instantly went into a pretend faint.

"Now you tell me you're going to take up sewing? Wonders will never cease!"

A remark that was *totally* uncalled for, considering she never even sews on a button if she thinks she can get away with a safety pin.

We left Mom and Benjy watching television and went upstairs to my bedroom. Needless to say, Mud had to come with us. He's the most extraordinarily inquisitive dog; he loves to know what's going on. Mom says it's a quest for grub. *I* say it's a sign of intelligence.

I knew where Mom kept the car rug: in a chest on the landing, along with a load of other stuff that she hardly ever uses.

"I don't think she'll even notice it's gone," I said.

Jilly and I aren't very good at sewing. In my case it is probably because Mom is so bad at it, which means it is hereditary and in my genes, and I just can't help it. But Jilly's mom does incredible embroidered cushion covers, so Jilly has no excuses. Yet she is just as useless as me!

It took us the whole evening to make our blanket for Daffodil, and even when we had finished, I could not honestly say that it was an object of beauty. Our stitches were all big and clumpy and uneven (and our fingers all pricked and bleeding).

"But it's not meant to be decorative," said Jilly. "It's more a practical kind of thing."

In case anyone ever wants to make a donkey blanket of their own, this is how we did it:

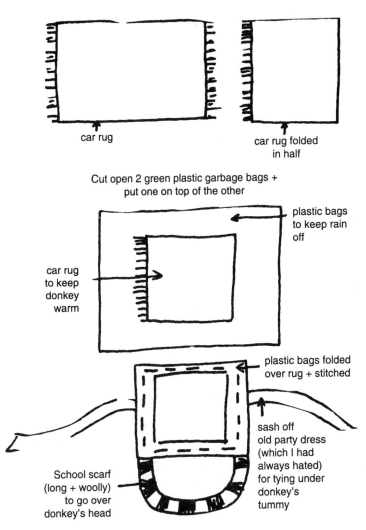

car rug

car rug folded in half

Cut open 2 green plastic garbage bags + put one on top of the other

plastic bags to keep rain off

car rug to keep donkey warm

plastic bags folded over rug + stitched

sash off old party dress (which I had always hated) for tying under donkey's tummy

School scarf (long + woolly) to go over donkey's head

We were really pleased with it!

"I just wish we could go and put it on her right now," I said. "I hate to think of her standing there all night in the cold."

We seriously considered stealing out of our beds in the dead of night, when everyone was asleep, and sneaking up to the Down, but Jilly was terrified that if her mom found out she would say she couldn't be an Animal Lover anymore, and I wasn't brave enough to go by myself. Besides, Mud would never let me get out of the house without barking.

If Mom hadn't been so stressed about her deadline, I might have asked her to drive us up there, but I just knew that in her present mood she would say no. *And* snap my head off.

"In any case," said Jilly, "she might see the car rug. And she'd certainly see your school scarf!"

Mom wasn't going to be happy about me using my school scarf to make a halter for Daffodil, but it was the only thing I'd been able to find that was long enough. It was great because it was thick and woolly, and would be a comfort to her.

"We'll go up there first thing after break-fast," said Jilly. "*First thing!*"

"I just hope she'll be all right," I said.

"Donkeys are hardy," said Jilly. "That horri-ble old man said so."

The wind raged all night long, and all night long I lay awake worrying about Daffodil. Nor-mally if the weather is wet or cold, I huddle close to Mud and feel a glow of satisfaction that he's safely tucked up in bed instead of drowning in a muddy ditch, but that night I could only think of poor Daffodil, shivering up on the Down. I kept repeating to myself that "Donkeys are *hardy*, donkeys are *hardy*," but it didn't stop me from worrying.

Next morning I was up and out of bed before Mom was even awake. I'd rolled up Daffodil's blanket and stuffed it into one of Mom's ordi-nary black garbage bags, and what I did was I went into the yard and dropped the sack over the back gate into the lane so that Mom wouldn't see me taking it out of the house and ask me what it was.

As soon as I'd had breakfast, I clipped Mud

on his leash and went around to Jilly's. Jilly came to the door still munching on her toast.

"Why aren't you ready?" I asked. I was desperate to get up to the Down and put Daffodil's blanket on her.

"I am, I'm coming," said Jilly. "I'm ready!"

Jilly went running back into the kitchen. I heard her mom say, "What's all the big rush? You haven't finished your breakfast."

"I'll eat it later!" cried Jilly, and she came scooting back into the hall, grabbed her jacket off its peg, stuffed her feet into her boots, and tore out through the front door before her mom could stop her.

"Oh! We haven't got any food," she said.

"I have," I told her. I'd raided the kitchen before Mom got out of bed. I'd put a plastic container full of goodies—bread and crackers and some oatmeal—in with the blanket. I'd thought of the oatmeal at the last minute. I'd heard of horses eating oats, so I thought perhaps donkeys would as well.

We zipped around the back and picked up the garbage bag, and I carried the bag and let Jilly

100

take Mud until he could safely be set loose, and we went galloping off toward Daffy Down. We'd decided to go by the road because of it being quicker, which meant that Jilly got to hold Mud's leash for a lot longer than usual, which I think she liked because it made her feel that she was in charge.

We reached Daffodil's field to find that she was standing in exactly the same place we had left her yesterday afternoon.

"Oh, Daffodil!" I cried, and I clambered over the fence and ran to her without even thinking about Jilly, left there with Mud on his leash.

Daffodil felt stiff all over, as if her bones had frozen. Her head was way down and even when I stroked her she didn't lift it.

"Quick!" I yelled to Jilly. "Come and help me!"

Jilly tied Mud to his tree—he was getting used to it by now—and hoisted herself over the fence. Between us, we unrolled Daffodil's blanket, slipped it over her head and settled it comfortably so that it covered her. Then we tied it in place and I started rubbing her legs, because I thought perhaps they were so cold that all the feeling had gone. While I was doing that, Jilly tried to feed her the food, but it was a long time before she would take any.

Then we were worried that she might be thirsty and couldn't get to her water, though even if she had been able to she wouldn't have been able to drink anything because there was a thick layer of ice on the top. The tub was really heavy, but we managed to tug and heave it over the frosty ground until it was near to her, and then we bashed at the ice and broke it.

It was all we could do. Even after all the trouble we'd gone to, stitching our fingers to the bone and pricking ourselves until we bled, it still didn't seem like very much.

"At least she's warm," said Jilly.

"A *little* warm."

"It's better than being freezing cold."

"Yes, but—" I clapped a hand to my mouth. I'd just thought of something. "Suppose the water gets ice on it again? She won't be able to drink!"

Jilly stopped, and looked at me. "What can we do?"

"I don't know! Maybe we could—could come up here again this afternoon and check."

It was all we could think of. We forgot about going to the shelter to help out: We just wanted to get back and make sure that Daffodil was all right.

"You're not taking that dog for *another* walk?" said Mom as I clipped Mud's leash on again around 3:00. "You were out for almost two hours this morning!"

"To make up for last Sunday," I begged. "He didn't go out at all, then."

"You're not still worried about your donkey, are you?" asked Mom. "I thought you told me that donkeys were hardy?"

"Yes, but we're scared her water will get ice over it," I said.

Mom just nodded. "All right, but don't be too long."

Daffodil still hadn't moved.

"Maybe she has but she keeps coming back again to the same place," said Jilly.

"Or maybe she's frozen and can't move," I said.

"She can't be *frozen*," said Jilly.

"Why can't she be?"

"Because—because she'd feel frozen. And she doesn't." Jilly slipped a hand under Daffodil's blanket. "She feels quite warm."

I slid my hand under, as well, and it was true: Daffodil *did* feel warm. That was some relief.

"She probably just likes this particular spot," said Jilly. "And we've given her some food and her water isn't frozen, so I think she'll be all right. After all, they're *hardy*."

That night wasn't as cold as Saturday night had been and so I didn't worry quite so much. I still woke up a few times, snuggled close to Mud, and thought about Daffodil in her bleak field, but it was a comfort to know that she had her nice waterproof coat and her warm woolly muffler.

On Monday morning, as I was leaving for school, Mom said to me, "Why aren't you wearing your scarf?"

"It's not cold enough yet," I said.

I didn't know what excuse I was going to make when it started to snow. But I thought that I would worry about that later.

Jilly's Animal Lovers badge had arrived, so at long last I was able to take mine out of my bag and pin it on the front of my sweater. Everyone at school (except, *of course*, Geraldine Hooper and No-Neck Puffin) was really impressed, and lots of people came up and wanted to know how they could get one.

One of the nicest things about wearing them was that Erik the Gorgeous saw them and came over to have a look. He said, "What's all this about?"

I was too scared to speak, but Jilly managed to stutter that they were "Animal Lovers badges . . . we're Animal Lovers. We help animals."

Erik said, "Great!" and we just nearly died. *Such* a pity Geraldine and No-Neck weren't there to hear it! It would have made them so-o-o-o jealous.

In spite of Daffodil having her warm blanket, we were still worried about her water freezing over because the weather was really cold, and we knew that horrible old Gristle wouldn't bother with her.

"He probably doesn't ever go out in this weather. *He* wouldn't care if she died of thirst."

"He isn't fit to keep a donkey," said Jilly. "He ought to be reported!"

"Maybe—" I stopped.

"Maybe what?" asked Jilly.

"Maybe we should . . . write to him."

"*Write* to him?" Jilly's face fell. "What good's that going to do?"

"We could threaten him! We could say that we'd report him to the RSPCA if he didn't start looking after Daffodil properly."

"Mm." Jilly didn't sound very convinced.

"They'd put him in prison, I bet! That'd scare him."

"Mm."

"Well, what else can we do?" I said.

Jilly suggested that before we wrote the letter we should try calling people again.

"Because it's no use thinking we can do *everything* by ourselves."

Of course there isn't any telephone in our school; not one that we can use. Only in the office, and then only if it's an emergency. We went there and tried telling Mrs. Southgate all about Daffodil and how she could be dying of thirst, but all Mrs. Southgate said was, "Not now, girls! I'm sorry, but I've got a million and one things to do. And it doesn't exactly sound as if it's an emergency."

Well! If one poor little donkey dying of thirst isn't an emergency, I'd like to know what is.

"When Geraldine Hooper broke her finger," said Jilly bitterly, "they called her mom up immediately. That was an emergency."

Jilly and I had to wait till we got home. Jilly said that, if I called the RSPCA, she would call Meg, but she called me after dinner to say that Meg and Denise were both out trying to rescue a dog that had been seen running along the railroad tracks. The girl who answered the phone was really dumb.

"I asked her about donkeys and all she said was, 'We've got two at the shelter, but they live here. They're not for adopting.' And then someone yelled at her and she said she had to go. How about you?" said Jilly. "Did you talk to the RSPCA?"

"Yes, but I got this woman," I said, "and she said there was another number I had to call. I've been trying and trying and it's just busy the whole time."

"It's always like that," said Jilly.

"I've decided," I said. "I'm going to write a letter."

"To the RSPCA?"

"To old Gristle. Are you going to come around and help me?"

Jilly sighed. "All right," she said.

We'd tried everything else, and we had to do *something*.

It took us a whole hour to work out our letter. It was quite difficult deciding what to say. In the end, this is what we wrote:

> *Rose Cottages,*
> *4 Honeypot Lane,*
> *Riddlestone*

Dear Mr. Grissom,

We are sorry but we do not think you are looking after your donkey properly. We think you are not giving her enough food, and the other day her water was frozen over so that she could not drink. Also she has no shelter and we think she ought to because she is like an old person and feels the cold. Another thing is that the field where she lives is dirty and horrible and we don't think it is right that she is kept in this mess.

If something is not done IMMEDIATELY *we are going to report you to the RSPCA.*

Yours faithfully,

(signed) Clara Carter

       Jilly Montague.

It was Jilly who made me write "We are sorry" at the beginning. She said it was what you did in letters.

"Even if you aren't sorry, it's what you put."

I was the one who wrote our address—well, *my* address—at the top and said that we should sign our names. Jilly didn't want us to. I think perhaps she was scared old Gristle would come after us, or something. But I told her how I'd once read that it was the act of a coward to send anonymous letters, and if we were going to be Animal Lovers fighting for animals, we couldn't afford to be cowards.

"We have to stand up and be counted."

So Jilly said all right, though I could see she still wasn't too happy about it.

After we'd finished I stole an envelope and a stamp from Mom, and put the letter in my schoolbag ready to mail on our way into school the next day. Old Gristle would get it on Wednesday.

"So by Wednesday night," said Jilly, "he ought to have done something."

We had to find a way of getting up there to check! We didn't dare leave it until the week-end. We knew that by the weekend it might be too late. Without food and water, poor Daffodil would not survive.

We racked our brains for a way of getting up to the Down. I suggested sneaking out again during the lunch recess on Thursday, but Jilly insisted we had to go before then.

"We've got to find out on Wednesday night!"

So we thought about it some more, and came up with the idea of telling Jilly's mom that we had to stay behind after school on that day and would be a bit late.

"Except suppose she asks why?"

"I'll say it's an after-school activity."

"Yes, but *what*?"

"I'll say it's a club. An animal club."

I stared at Jilly in awe. Jilly never *ever* tells lies to her mom. Not real big whopping lies like that.

She tossed her head.

"What's your problem? It is a club! Animal Lovers. That's a club."

Well, it was, sort of. I mean, we'd paid money to join, hadn't we?

"OK," I said.

So that was what we decided to do. The reason it was only Jilly's mom we had to tell, and not mine, was that Wednesday was the day of Mom's deadline for the aluminum and she was going to take it up to the agency herself, and while she was in London she was going to do some Christmas shopping and wasn't going to be back until maybe 6:00, so Mrs. Montague had agreed that I could go back with Jilly. Benjy was going to stay with one of his friends, and poor Mud was going to be left on his own. I felt terrible about this, but Mom promised she would take him for a walk before she went out.

"He's got to get used to being left alone sometimes."

When we woke up on Wednesday it was really horrible: all gray and cold with a sleety rain. Mom said I was stupid not to wear my scarf.

"No one's going to give you any medals for being tough."

Jilly was wearing hers because her mom had made her. Halfway to school she insisted that I had to have it. She said it was because we were friends, "and friends share." She also said that her mom had offered to come and pick us up after school to save us walking home in the cold.

"Oh no!" I said. "What did you say?"

"I told her we liked walking and that people shouldn't pick their children up from school in cars because it was bad for the environment. She said I was crazy," said Jilly. "And now we'll have to walk there and back every single day even if it *snows*!"

"It's all for a good cause," I said. "It's all for animals."

As soon as school was let out we took to our heels and ran like the wind. It was quicker without Mud, because if he's off the leash you have to keep waiting for him while he investigates things, and if he's on the leash you can't run properly.

We got there in 15 minutes flat, which must, I think, be a record. But we were shocked at what we saw: The field was empty. Daffodil was gone!

Chapter 8

"Oh!" Jilly's voice trembled and broke. "Where is she?"

"Where is she?"

"She's not here!"

"Where's she gone?"

"I don't know!"

We looked at each other, our eyes wide with anguish.

"Maybe . . . he came and took her away."

"Took her where?"

"To a stable!"

"Old Gristle?"

It didn't seem very likely, but it was all I could think of.

Actually, that's not true. There was something else I could think of, only it was too upsetting and so I was trying not to.

Unfortunately, Jilly went ahead and said it.

"Oh, Clara!" Her bottom lip had started to wobble. "You don't think she died, do you?"

I had to swallow about three times before I could trust myself to speak.

"She had her coat," I said.

"But she was old!"

I thought of poor Daffodil, dying all by herself in her bleak field, with no one to hold her or comfort her, and I felt the tears welling in my eyes.

"We ought to go and ask him," I said.

"We can't!" sobbed Jilly. "We've got to get back!"

I knew that she was right. Jilly's mom, and my mom, too, would be *really* furious if we stayed out after dark. They would never let us go anywhere again, ever. We would be banned from taking Mud for walks, banned from going to the shelter: We wouldn't be able to do anything at all to help animals. Not, I reflected miserably, that we had done very much to help Daffodil.

"We should have made someone listen," I said.

Jilly rubbed her eyes. "We'll know better next time."

"Yes, but it's too late for Daffodil!"

One of the worst things was that we couldn't tell anyone. We couldn't say to Mom, when she arrived home, that we were worried about Daffodil because she had disappeared. She would immediately want to know how we knew this, and then we would have to confess that we had lied to Jilly's mom, and once again we would be in trouble. *Mega* trouble. And obviously, for the same reason, we couldn't talk about it to Jilly's mom, not that she would have been sympathetic. Not properly. She is not an animal person.

"She wouldn't ever *hurt* one," Jilly said to me earnestly.

"Apart from bashing flies," I said.

"Oh, well, yes, but lots of people do that. Yours probably would if Mud didn't get to them first."

This was true and so I didn't say any more. I was already feeling awful enough, without starting an argument with Jilly.

"If only we *knew*," I said.

I sometimes think that being 11 is one of the worst ages to be. It is old enough to be upset by all the terrible things that go on in the world, and to feel that you must try and do something that will stop them from happening, but not old enough for grown-ups to just let you get on with it. All the time they are telling you what you can do and what you cannot do and making it extremely difficult for you to do anything at all.

Jilly and I couldn't even do a simple thing like going to see old Gristle and asking about Daffodil! It wasn't that we minded our moms being mad at us—well, we did mind, but you have to get used to that sort of thing when you are fighting battles, just as you have to get used to people making fun of you, or groaning and being impatient. What scared us was in case they said we couldn't be Animal Lovers anymore.

"We can't even go and talk to him on Saturday," moaned Jilly, " 'cause your mom will be there."

I thought that on Saturday Mom would probably come with us to see old Gristle if we asked her, but Saturday was too late. I couldn't wait until Saturday! We had to find out *now*.

Jilly's mom was in a really good mood, all chatty and wanting to know what our "animal club" was about.

"Oh! Just . . . finding out about animals," said Jilly.

"Will you be going on expeditions? To the Bird Sanctuary and places?"

"Um . . . yes. Maybe. I suppose so."

"And the zoo? We took you to the zoo when you were a little girl. Do you remember?"

Jilly said, "Yes. Only we don't really approve of zoos now."

"Oh, don't tell me! You don't like to see animals in cages."

"We think it's cruel," said Jilly. "Don't we?"

Jilly signaled frantically at me across the table, but I was too busy thinking of a way to find out about Daffodil and wasn't very much help to her. In fact, I wasn't any help at all.

I heard Jilly's mom tell her that she hadn't minded seeing the animals in their cages when she was little, and I heard Jilly say, "Yes, but

I'm older, now." Then I suddenly heard myself blurting out, "Would it be all right if we just went next door to see Mud for a few minutes? He's been on his own for ages."

"Not that long," said Mrs. Montague. "Your mom didn't leave here until noon."

"Yes, but that's still . . ." I did some hasty finger work under the table. "That's still over four hours!"

"Well, you can go and see him if you like, but you'll only start him barking."

"We could bring him back here," said Jilly. "Couldn't we, Mom? Please!"

Jilly's mom has this strange thing about animals, that they shouldn't ever come into people's houses, but for once she relented and said all right, we could bring him, but we were to make sure that his feet were clean.

She was in a *really* good mood!

The reason I'd wanted to go around to my place wasn't only to see Mud. There was another reason, as well. I told it to Jilly on the doorstep, because I knew the minute we opened the door Mud would be all over us, yipping and yelping, and we wouldn't be able to hear ourselves think.

"We could look up old Gristle's number in the telephone book and then we could call him."

"Oh! Great idea," said Jilly.

Obviously, we couldn't have done it from Jilly's house in case her mom heard us. So I said that I would look up the number while Jilly took Mud into the front yard in case he wanted to do something (I knew her mom would go ballistic if he piddled in hers).

I looked under every spelling of Grissom I could think of—one s, two s's, even with a *y*—but he wasn't in there. Old Gristle didn't have a telephone!

I must have looked really down because Jilly said kindly that I had done my best.

"Whoever heard of anyone not having a telephone?"

Before we went back to Jilly's place, I thought I would pick up a handful of dog biscuits for Mud. I went out to the kitchen—and froze.

"Jilly!" I shrieked.

"What?" Jilly came running, with Mud as

usual doing his best to trip her up.

"Look!"

There on the kitchen table was Daffodil's blanket . . .

We just couldn't imagine how it had gotten there. We went back to Jilly's place and took Mud up to Jilly's bedroom (Mrs. Montague wouldn't have him in the kitchen because she didn't think it was hygienic!) and tried to settle down to our homework, but there was just no way that either of us could concentrate. Every few minutes one of us would say "Maybe . . ." or "Perhaps . . ." and then stop, because we really couldn't think maybe or perhaps *what*.

All we knew was that wherever she was, poor Daffodil no longer had on her nice warm blanket.

"I just hope," sobbed Jilly, "that he hasn't done anything horrible to her!"

We both had this fear that our letter might have made him so angry he'd gone and sold Daffodil to the slaughterhouse to be turned into dog food.

"But then," I said, scrubbing my nose on my

sleeve, "why would he bother bringing the blanket back?"

"To gloat," said Jilly, and we both hugged Mud and wept tears into his fur.

By the time Mom arrived home, we were both red eyed and blotchy.

"Mom!" I went racing down the stairs, with Mud and Jilly hot on my heels. "Why is Daffodil's blanket on the kitchen table?"

"*Daffodil's* blanket?" said Mom. "I thought it was my car rug!"

But she could see that Jilly and I were in a state, and so she relented and said, "It's a long story, girls, but Daffodil is safe. At least, she's being cared for."

Because Jilly was obviously as desperate as I was to hear what had happened, Mrs. Montague actually let us all—including Mud!—go and sit down in her living room, where Mom told the tale.

She had taken Mud for his walk, and was just about to make herself a cup of coffee when there was this loud hammering at the door and it was old Gristle, all red and raging, saying how he'd had a disrespectful letter from Jilly and me telling him he wasn't looking after his donkey properly. He'd said that as far as he was concerned we could "very well have the bloomin' old donkey." He washed his hands of it; it was nothing but a darned nuisance, anyway.

"He told me," said Mom, "that if we wanted it we'd better get it off his property immediately before he changed his mind. You did a good job, you two! You really stirred up a hornets' nest."

"They sure took matters into their own hands, didn't they?" That was Jilly's mom, thinking that perhaps we'd done something we shouldn't. But Mom stuck up for us!

"They didn't really have much choice," she said, and she made a face, sort of guilty and apologetic. "I haven't been too good at listening lately, have I? I knew they were worried about Daffodil; I should have paid more attention. In the end, they did the only thing they could—and according to Meg, it was just as well."

"Oh! Is she with Meg?" I cried.

Mom said yes, she'd driven out to the shelter

at once to tell them. Meg had immediately jumped into her horsevan and driven up to Daffy Down with Denise.

"Denise came around with the blanket just before I left for town. She said she and Meg had been absolutely horrified; they'd never seen a donkey in such terrible condition. They took her back to the shelter right there and then, and called the vet out to have a look at her."

"Is she going to be all right?" begged Jilly.

"Well . . ." Mom hesitated. "She's a very sick little donkey."

The tears spurted into my eyes. "We let it go too long!"

"No." Mom took hold of my hands. "You and Jilly did everything you possibly could. It wasn't your fault if I didn't listen to you. If you want to blame anyone, then blame me."

"Blame old Gristle!" said Jilly.

"Well, yes, he was certainly guilty of appalling neglect. Meg says you were right to threaten him."

I could see Jilly's mom looking a bit alarmed at this.

"He showed me the letter," said Mom. "It was actually quite polite—and extremely well written! Not a single spelling mistake."

I tried to smile, but I couldn't. I was too worried about what was going to happen to Daffodil.

"Look," said Mom, "she's in good hands, she's being taken care of. If anyone can pull her through, it's Meg. I thought, if you like, I'll pick you both up after school tomorrow. If that's all right with Jilly's mom?" Jilly's mom nodded. "Then we can drive out and see how she is. Would you like to do that?"

"Yes, please," I whispered. Jilly didn't say anything. I don't think she could speak. We were very relieved, of course, that poor Daffodil wasn't up on the Down anymore, shivering and cowering in her horrible dump of a field, but we knew from the grave expression on Mom's face that Daffodil still might die.

We couldn't wait for it to be the end of school so that we could go and visit her. Mom was waiting for us as she'd promised. She had Benjy with her and she had obviously told him that we were going to visit a sick little donkey because he kept chanting, "Dick iddle dongy. Baw, Daddledill!" I tried not to let it get on my nerves. I knew it was his way of showing that he cared. But it was extremely irritating!

When we reached the shelter, Meg said that Daffodil was still very sick, but that Jilly and I could go and talk to her.

"She knows your voices. It might buck her up a bit, give her the will to go on fighting."

Daffodil was lying in a stable on a thick bed of straw and covered with a proper donkey blanket. She looked so peaceful, but Meg explained that that was only because she was too weak to move. She said that the vet had given her a vitamin injection, and she was being fed a mixture of milk and glucose.

We stroked her and whispered to her—"Please, Daffodil! Please get better"—but we cried on our way home because we were so upset.

The next day was Friday and Meg called Mom to say the vet didn't hold out much hope. She said that, if Jilly and I wanted to come and say good-bye to Daffodil, we should do it that day because she might not last another 24 hours.

Mom picked us up again after school, and Jilly and I both cried when she told us what Meg had said.

Denise met us at the entrance and she was crying, too. She said, "I know I ought to be used to it by now, but I just hate it when we lose an animal."

Meg was waiting for us in the stable.

"I'm afraid she's sinking," she said. "We've done all we could, but she was just too far gone. She hasn't moved all night. She can't even eat the hay we've put down for her. But I'll leave you on your own for a few minutes. You can say good-bye in your own way."

Jilly and I crouched by Daffodil's side. The tears were streaming down our faces. It was difficult to believe this was the same little donkey who had hung her big furry head over the fence and nuzzled our hands for food.

"Oh Daffodil!" I whispered. "Darling Daffodil! I'm sorry!"

"It was all our fault," sobbed Jilly. "We should have done something sooner!"

"Sweet, darling Daffodil," I wept.

"Just a poor little innocent donkey." Jilly rubbed her cheek, all wet with tears, against Daffodil's. "A poor little innocent donkey that never did anyone any harm."

"It's so unfair!"

Very, very gently, we stroked her neck. A long, shuddering sigh ran through her. Her poor thin ribs heaved and her wasted flanks shuddered. I honestly, truly thought that she had gone.

"Oh, Daffodil!"

We had failed her. We called ourselves Animal Lovers and we had let this little donkey down. It wasn't any use saying that we would know better in the future. In the future was too late. All I cared about was *now*—and Daffodil.

And then the strangest thing happened. There was this weird, unearthly sound—a sort of wheezing and braying and rasping—and there were these two donkey heads looming over the door of the stable. Doris and Bert! What were they doing here?

They brayed, in unison. "Ee-aw! Ee-aw!" And slowly, ever so slowly, ever so painfully,

Daffodil raised her head. Her eyes were clouded, and yet she had responded! Without even stopping to think, I snatched up a handful of sweet-smelling hay and offered it to her. But her head sank back, and it seemed as if she was just too weak.

"Oh, Daffodil," I whispered. "Please try!"

Ee-aw, ee-aw, went Doris and Bert.

And Daffodil lifted her head, just inches, that was all, but her lips were making those funny, pouting movements that meant she was interested. She wanted some food!

I started to feed it to her, bit by tiny bit.

"Go and get Meg!" I hissed. "Tell her she's eating!"

Oh, and that was the turning point! From that moment on, Daffodil slowly started to get better. Meg said, "She must have recognized you. You gave her the will to live!"

But it wasn't us. It was Doris and Bert!

Denise said, "It was the most extraordinary thing! I opened the gate of the field and they both came pushing past me, out into the yard, and headed straight for the stable. Almost as if they knew! As if they wanted to encourage her."

"They did!" said Jilly. "It was all thanks to them!"

"Which just goes to show," said Meg, "that animals understand a great deal more than we humans realize."

When we went to visit Daffodil on Saturday, Denise gave us a gooey mixture of bran and molasses to feed her, and by Sunday she was actually standing up, though still a bit wobbly.

Bert and Doris had been to see her again, and Meg said she was hoping they would befriend her and form a little group. She told us that donkeys are in fact extremely sociable animals and that there is almost nothing more cruel than keeping one all by itself. She also told us that poor Daffodil must have been neglected for years and it was a miracle she had survived.

We learned from Meg that of course donkeys need shelter and proper food—not just scraps, which was what horrible old Gristle had been feeding her. She said that our rolls and carrots had probably been a lifesaver.

"And the coat, as well. She must have suffered terribly being up on the Down in the freezing cold."

As for her deformed feet, Meg almost exploded when we told her how Gristle had said it was natural.

"Natural! It most certainly is not! The poor little creature is half crippled!"

She explained how donkeys need their hooves trimmed regularly, preferably every eight weeks, and that they should never be left to stand all day in a muddy, dirty field as Daffodil had been.

"It could have done permanent damage. It's just downright, willful ignorance! People should not have animals if they can't be bothered to learn how to look after them properly."

Jilly said, "We didn't know how they should be looked after. We should have found out."

"You did what you could," said Meg. "You actually talked to her owner. You could not know he was deceiving you. I have nothing but praise for you both! If it weren't for you, this poor old lady would have been dead by now.

Not that she's as old as all that. With any luck, now she's with us, she'll go on for another 20 years."

Jilly and I were amazed! Daffodil could live to see us leaving school, and growing up and starting a shelter of our very own.

"But I think she should always stay here," I said, "because she's got her friends."

We all went to see her one week later, Jilly and me, and Mom and Benjy. Her hooves had been trimmed and she was out in the field with Doris and Bert, and the two goats, Petal and Tulip, and the old horse, Captain. Meg said that Doris and Bert were being very protective toward her and wouldn't let her out of their sight. They were all going around in a threesome as if they were old buddies, nodding up and down with their heads together.

We called to Daffodil, and she flung up her head immediately and gave her funny wheezing call—"Ee-aw! Ee-aw!"—and set off toward us. She couldn't gallop yet, and maybe she would never be able to because of being mistreated for so long, but at least she could walk without being in pain. As she came near to us she even broke into a little trot!

"It's so rewarding," said Meg, "isn't it? When you think what she was like at the beginning of the week . . . I really thought we were going to lose her."

We stayed at the shelter for over an hour, talking to Daffodil (who was going to be a permanent resident) and looking at all the other animals who were waiting for homes.

I kept saying, "Oh Mom! Look! Look, Mom!" in the hope that I might tempt her into taking one back with us, but I think she guessed what I was up to because in the end she said, "I think we ought to leave now before you try saddling me with a donkey or a goat or half a dozen cats. I must warn you, Clara . . . I have decided: No more animals! One is quite enough."

Oh, ha ha! That's what she thinks!

Look for *Snow Kittens,* also in the We Love Animals Series.

Snow Kittens

When we went into school the following morning and George Handley started threatening us with all the things he was going to do ("You wait til I get you two alone!"), I couldn't help trembling just a little bit and wondering if perhaps our moms had been right, but George Handley is all mouth, he never did any of the things he threatened. And—(this is the really good part!)—if it hadn't been for me and Jilly letting them have it for being cruel, Darren Bickerstaff might never have told us about the kittens.

I'm not saying I care more about kittens than snails . . . well, perhaps I *do*, because who can help it? Kittens are so sweet! I'm afraid you can't really say that about snails. I mean, you can't really get a close relationship going with a snail. Not as far as I know. But the kittens were to make this huge, enormous mega change in Jilly's mom. Up until then, Jilly's mom had been dead set against having animals in the house. Nasty, dirty things! Dropped hairs everywhere, full of fleas, ugh! Horrible.

Then, suddenly—

Bingo! It all changed. Nobody was more surprised than me and Jilly.

This is how it happened.

It was about a month after the snail incident. The end of November, really cold and dark and gloomy. We'd just had a load of snow. Everyone kept saying, "Snow! In November!" Like it doesn't normally happen then. Maybe it doesn't; I can't remember. But this year it did and it was fre-e-e-e-ezing.

One Saturday, when we were out walking Mud, we bumped into Darren Bickerstaff. Well, we didn't actually bump into him. First, we saw him in the distance with George Handley and the rest of the gang. Jilly said, "Let's go the other way." So we grabbed Mud and set off fast in the opposite direction. But the next thing we know, Darren's running after us yelling, "Hey! You two!"

"Run!" hissed Jilly.

We really thought he was going to get us, work us over, because of the snails. I prodded at Mud to get his attention (he'd gone and put his head down a hole, and of course he can't hear, no matter how loud you shout), and we hurried off. But Darren's a really fast runner and he's much bigger than us, and before very long his feet were pounding hotly behind us.

"What you running for?" he cried. "I got somethin' to tell you! 'Bout animals!"

That made us stop. We turned and faced him. I held on tight to Mud's collar, just in case. I mean, in case Darren made a snatch at him or something. Mud wouldn't harm a fly!

Actually, that's not quite true: He eats flies. But he'd never harm a human being.

"So what is it?" I asked.

"I know where there's a cat that's just had kittens . . . up on the golf course. I think it's dead."

"So why tell us?" wailed Jilly. Jilly can't bear dead things. I'm not too happy with them myself. But Jilly goes into floods if she sees, like, a poor squashed fox on the road.

"Cause it might not be dead," said Darren. "And it's got these kittens an' all. You wanna come an' see?"

We looked at each other. I could tell Jilly was thinking what I was thinking: It's got to be some kind of practical joke.

"Is this your idea of a joke?" I asked.

"No! Honest! It's up there. I was gonna tell someone, but then I saw you. I thought you'd know what to do," said Darren. "Being into animals an' that."

I made a decision. There are times when you have to take a chance.

"OK," I said. "Show us!"

"It better not be some kind of a trick," said Jilly.

"It ain't," said Darren.

And it wasn't. He led us up onto the golf course, all covered in snow, and there, in a nest among some bushes, was this pathetic mother cat and her kittens. She must have been so beautiful! She was pure white and so were the kittens. Four of them, in all. Little, sad bundles of fur. Jilly couldn't bear it. She took one look and just dissolved, so I gave her Mud to hold while I knelt down in the snow.

"They're dead, ain't they?" said Darren.

I wasn't sure. I knew that this time I had to be *really* brave. Braver, even, than when we'd rescued the snails. I forced myself to reach out a hand and feel the mother cat. It's terrible feeling an animal when the life has gone out of it, and it's all stiff and cold. But I made myself do it. And then I felt the kittens, very carefully, one by one.

"I think two of them might still be alive," I said.

"Really? You think?"

"They are!" I said. "They're still breathing!"

Darren's face lit up. Just for a moment he looked like a really nice boy. Not in the least like a boy who would chuck stones at snails.

"What'll we do?" he said.

"Rescue them!"

I ripped off my scarf, which was long and woolly. Then I picked up the two little white bundles and wrapped them in it.

"Here!" I thrust them at Darren. He seemed a bit taken aback.

"You want me to have 'em?"

"Just til we get home. Put them in your jacket! They've got to be kept warm."

Darren is quite big and chunky, whereas I am rather small and weedy. Also, he was wearing a big thick sweater and a down jacket, so I thought it would probably be cozier for the kittens in there than in my jacket.

"Come on!" I said. "Quick! Let's get back home!"